INDIAN CHILD

Other books by the author:

The Devil's Missionary, 1997

Planned for future publication:

Hunter of Men
Hunter of Men II
Restless Love
Terror by Night
Worth to be Loved
The House of Rue
The Kaiser House
The Awakened
Little Feather

INDIAN CHILD

JAMES B. FLOOK

LUTHERS
New Smyrna Beach
FLORIDA

FIRST EDITION
Copyright © 2002 by James B. Flook
ALL RIGHTS RESERVED

No part of this book may be reproduced or transmitted in any form or by any means—including photocopying, recording or by an information storage or retrieval system—without written permission from the publisher, except for brief quotations used in reviews.

Published by
LUTHERS PUBLISHING
1009 North Dixie Freeway
New Smyrna Beach, FL 32168-6221
www.lutherspublishing.com

PRINTED IN THE UNITED STATES OF AMERICA

LIBRARY OF CONGRESS
CATALOGING-IN-PUBLICATION DATA
Flook, James B., 1927–
Indian child / James B. Flook.—1st ed.
p. cm.
ISBN 1-877633-66-6
1. Overland journeys to the Pacific—Fiction.
2. Wagon trains—Fiction. 3. Indian girls—Fiction.
4. Orphans—Fiction.
I. Title.

PS3556.L5828 I5 2002
813'.54—dc21   2002041038

*To my two daughters
Susan and Kay*

*To Evelynne Chambers
for her encouragement*

✣✣✣✣✣✣✣✣ CHAPTER ONE ✣✣✣✣✣✣✣✣

HANNIBAL, MISSOURI—1865. The war was over and the streets were clogged with battered soldiers from both the North and South, heading West, and a new life. They were challenging the unknown, but for most of them, nothing could be more like hell than what they had just gone through.

As one ragged young Yankee soldier put it. "I'll always see the battle and smell the blood. It will be with me as long as I walk the battlefields that lay in every valley and in every forest laid waste by artillery fire. I must leave or I'll go mad."

Ward Taylor, a young blonde haired man with a full mustache, walked slowly down a dusty street leading a sleek black stallion. Much like other cavalrymen, at the time of his muster he kept the horse that had been assigned to him. To help remove the stench of war from his mind and body he had taken a bath then destroyed his uniform.

After replacing his uniform with clean new clothes from the skin out, he topped it off with a new mountaineer sombrero with a flat crown and a wide leather band. He didn't know if it was because of the dark days that had just passed that forced him to buy black clothing, or if he just wanted to separate himself completely from the military. Regardless of the reason, he carried himself with pride. His country had called him and he answered the call to defend her.

Reaching the end of main street, Ward came upon a marshalling area where wagon trains were being assembled to go West. People, cattle, oxen, mules and horses all mingled together. It was like a melting pot during the off loading of a ferry that had just docked. Other ferries setting off shore in the mighty Mississippi were waiting to be unloaded. The world for most of them had stopped during the war, but now they were heading West. Eagerly they sought a new life. Loud voices boomed as the wagon masters ordered those who would be following them to the West Coast, to get their belongings around and line up in an orderly fashion. Women and children scurried around and climbed into their wagons.

Ward looked over the various trains being assembled, then he approached a large red faced wagon master. "Get out of here kid," shouted the man. "If you don't have a wagon then move on."

Ward snapped his Smith and Wesson from its holster and shoved it into the wagon master's belly. "No one, but no one calls me a kid. I've killed more men face to face than you could ever imagine."

The wagon master extended his hand. A broad smile peered out from under his bushy mustache. "Sorry young man, I can see it in your eyes, you've done some killin'."

"You bet I have....Guess I'm a bit touchy about being called a kid, but I can see this is no place for a boy." With that, Ward holstered his iron and shook hands with the wagon master.

The grip was firm. "They call me Hawk; the name is Hawkshaw, but I never answer to that."

"Ward Taylor here."

"Glad to meet you, Ward. Got a wagon with you?"

"No, I'm traveling alone and light."

"I can use a good man with a gun and a fine horse like you got there."

"What do I have to do?"

"I need a fearless scout and I think you're just the man I'm looking for." replied Hawk, patting Ward's horse on the jawbone.

"What's it pay?" asked Ward.

"You want to get to California?" growled Hawk.

"That's what I'm here for."

"Then that's your pay. I have all the supplies you and I will need, so all you have to have is a bedroll, your side arm and that sleek young stallion. What do you say to that?"

Ward thought for a moment. Realizing it would not cost

him a thing to get to the West Coast and that he would still have all of his muster pay, he reached for Hawk's hand. "It's a deal."

Hawk raised his right fist into the air. "You won't be sorry. Now promise me one thing."

"What's that?" countered Ward.

"That you will not go with another train."

"I shook on the deal, didn't I?"

"Well—yes."

"That's my word and I am a man of my word."

Hawk smiled. "Damn if I don't believe you."

Ward stroked his horse's mane. "What do you want me to do?"

"Just get some rest, you'll need it."

"When we leaving?" asked Ward

"Day after tomorrow."

"I'll be here," said Ward, turning away.

"By the way, Ward, what was your unit?"

"Michigan 4th Cavalry."

"Guess that says it all," said Hawk, rubbing his wiry beard.

"You have heard of us?"

"Oh, yes, Ward, I have heard of your unit." With that, Hawk's booming voice echoed among the people, nearly stampeding the animals.

Ward left the marshalling area and returned to the main street, there to be among those who were loading their wagons with supplies for the grueling trip West. He noticed there were a lot of young people willing to risk their lives for a better life for themselves and the children that were clinging to their mother's skirts.

Young women, scantly dressed, sat on an upstairs porch railing of one of the hotels overlooking the main street. Ward caught one of their wondering eyes, but didn't respond to her act of pushing her thin dress tie off her shoulder, nearly bearing herself to the waist.

Ward couldn't help but see the nods and hear the comments being made about his sleek black stallion. Pride surged through Ward's veins for he and his horse had gone to hell and back several times during the war. Ward considered his horse as family for he was the only living thing

Ward thought he could trust.

Tying his horse to a hitching post, Ward moved slowly along the boardwalk. Coming upon a saloon filled with people enjoying themselves, he had a thought come to mind. He couldn't remember the last time he'd laughed out loud. With a slight grin on his face, he pushed aside the swinging door and muscled his way to the bar. A massive back bar, hand carved in the finest detail stood behind the bartender. A large mirror reflected the many bottles of whiskey setting on the back bar. "Give me a whiskey," shouted Ward, over the clamor of the jovial crowd.

Ward had drank about half of his drink when someone elbowed him in the ribs. "You sure look like a dude to me with all that fancy black on."

Ward turned, facing the man. "A dude you say?"

"That's what I said."

"And just what is that suppose to mean?" inquired Ward, stepping back as far as he could against the crowd.

"I guess it's suppose to mean that anyone dressing like that is some kind of a sissy."

With a left hand, quick as a fox's paw, Ward planted a hand full of knuckles in the stranger's face, slamming him against the bar. When he came forward, Ward sent out a wicked right, catching the stranger squarely on the chin. The stranger's tongue flopped outside his mouth. His head dropped and he fell in a heap on the floor.

A red-eyed old fellow, barely sober enough to hang onto the bar slobbered a remark, "Thank ya son for that, he ain't been nothing but trouble ever since he walked through the door." The old man hiccuped then turned, facing the bar once more.

Ward's eyes shifted from one patron to another, just looking for someone to challenge him again.

"The next drink is on the house, young man," shouted the bartender.

Ward nodded and smiled before reaching for his glass setting on the bar.

The bartender leaned over the bar and pointed to the man still laying on the floor. "Will some of you drag his mange carcass out of here and throw him into the street. I haven't got time for the likes of him."

While two of the customers were dragging the man out who had fallen in the wake of Ward's lightning hands, the red-eyed old man turned around once more. Looking down at Ward's hands, he mumbled, "Ain't never saw a pair of hands as fast as the ones you got hanging from your arms."

Ward smiled. "I don't know if I should thank you for that or not."

"No need for that young man, I was just stating a fact. When I was young I would have taken ya on, but I know you would have whipped me just like you did that feller going out the door."

"Now we don't know that do we?" said Ward, stepping over to where the old man was standing.

"No, I guess we don't, so let's just say it would have been a hell of a fight." replied the old man, smiling through his ragged tobacco stained teeth.

Ward could hardly stand the smell of the old gentlemen, but still there was something that attracted Ward to him. "Where you going?" asked Ward, downing his last swallow and placing his glass on the bar for a refill.

"This one is on me," said the bartender.

"It don't need to be," replied Ward.

The bartender looked out from under his brow while pouring Ward's drink. "Where I'm standing there is nothing I have to do, but when I want to do something, I do it."

"I hear what you're saying and thanks," smiled Ward, reaching for his glass and pulling it to him.

"You asked where I was going?" said the old man.

"Yes, I did."

"I was going West, but this is as far as I got," replied the old man, dropping his eyes and looking down at the glass he held in his hand.

"You going out with one of the trains tomorrow?" asked Ward, looking into the old man's wasted eyes.

"Nope. Sure would like to, but I know no one wants an old man holding them up. A trip like that is for the young. I'll just stay here and die."

Ward glanced at the bartender. The bartender nodded his head then went on about his way.

The old man looked up at Ward. "When you get to be my age, nobody wants you around, because they think we can't hold up our end."

"Can you?" asked Ward, leaning on one elbow and looking into the old man's reddened eyes.

"Hold up my end? Just let someone give me a chance and I'll show 'em I can."

"Can you handle a team of mules?" asked Ward, still looking at the old man who had dropped his eyes once more and stood scuffing the brass rail with his foot.

"Can I handle a team of mules?" boasted the old man. "Dang if I wasn't the best mule skinner in the war."

"You were?"

"Yep. I weren't no good for fightin' no more, but that didn't stop me from doing my part."

"Where you from?" asked Ward.

"West Virginia."

"Which side did you fight on?"

"I bet you'll be all done talking to me, but it was the south."

Ward smiled and placed his hand on the old man's shoulder. "Were you in the war because you felt you were right?"

"Well, of course I was."

"So was I and isn't that the only thing that's important?"

The old man dumped his last swallow. "Damn if you ain't a smart young man and I suppose you were fighting for the north."

"That's right and does that make any difference to you?"

The old man smiled, "It would have before I met you."

Ward extended his hand to the old man and was met with a rather spunky remark. After the old man jerked his hand back he said, "You don't want to be touching me. I'm as dirty as the rats that run the streets."

Ward grabbed the old man's hand and shook it. "You can wash away the dirt, old timer, but in a lifetime when we meet a good man we must count ourselves lucky"

"You mean me?" asked the old man.

"Yes, I mean you," replied Ward.

"Gee, I ain't been told I'm worth anything in so long I don't know what to say."

Ward shifted his weight from the brass rail to the floor. "Would you still like to go West?"

"Well, heck yes, I'd still like to go West, but that ain't going to happen."

"I'll make a deal with you...." Ward hesitated, "What's your name?"

"They call me Leaky and that's all I want to be known by."

"All right Leaky, I'm going to take you down to the boardinghouse and you're going to take a bath, then we are heading for the river where you can meet Hawk."

"A bath! And who's Hawk?"

"Yes, a bath and Hawk is the man responsible for getting us to the West Coast."

"How come you know him?" asked Leaky.

"I just hired on as a scout."

"You did?"

"That's right."

"And what good do you think I'd be on a trip out there?"

Ward's face became serious. "I think you'd have a lot to offer, but it's all up to Hawk. He's the man we have to satisfy."

"Can't we just go see this Hawk feller first?"

"No," insisted Ward. "You're going to take a bath and you're going to trim that beard of yours."

"Why so?" exclaimed Leaky.

"Because you would scare the life out of all the prairie dogs if you went out there looking like you do."

Reluctantly Leaky agreed and they started out the door. "Oh, by the way," said Ward, "can you go without your whiskey? I don't think they would have room for that."

"To get out to California, I'd go without sleep."

Ward smiled. "Then let's get you to the boardinghouse."

CHAPTER TWO

WARD WITH LEAKY at his side, left for the boardinghouse. There he saw to it that Leaky was clean and that he had trimmed his ragged beard. He wasn't a fashion plate when Ward got through with him, but he did look a hundred percent better than he did when Ward met him in the saloon.

On the way to the marshaling area Leaky said, "You sure this Hawk feller is going to let me go with him to the West Coast?"

"I can't guarantee you that, but I'm betting if you play your cards right he will let you go."

"I don't know about that," mumbled Leaky.

"Now if Hawk sounds like he doesn't want you as part of his crew, you just come right back at him and tell him why you think you would add something to the trip."

"Gee, I don't know about that. I ain't much for tooting my own horn."

"You can handle mules, right?"

"Yep."

"What else can you do?"

"I can cook."

Ward swallowed hard. It was difficult for him to think of Leaky being a cook and working around food. "There you see," insisted Ward. "You have two important things you can do, now let's find Hawk."

"How well do you know this feller?" asked Leaky, rubbing his lips with one finger.

"Just met him not more than a few hours ago."

"Well, heck sakes, you don't know him either."

"You're right, but I do have a job with him."

"That's right you do," Leaky hesitated. "Let's go see this

Hawk feller."

Leaky was a small wiry man who appeared to be as tough as a piece of dried rawhide. His face was lined and his eyes were piercing. His hats wide brim was turned up in front and laid tightly against the crown. His arms hung at his sides and appeared to be cocked at the elbows. They made a sweeping motion as he swaggered along with Ward, heading for the location where Hawk was assembling his followers.

Leaky, puffing some, spoke up, "Never seen so darn many people and animals in my life. How we going to find Hawk?"

"He can't be very far," replied Ward.

Only minutes had passed when Ward stopped and put his hand across Leaky's chest. "Did you hear that?"

"Hear what? There's so darn much noise I couldn't pick one noise out from another."

"You can this one. Do you hear that loud shouting voice?"

"Well, yes, I can hear that."

"That's Hawk all right, now let's keep going."

Ward lead the way, pushing through the mass of people. Finally they stopped and there in front of him stood Hawk directing the activities at hand. "Hawk," shouted Ward.

"Ya, what is it?"

"It's me, Ward."

"I thought I told you to get some rest."

"You did and that's what I'm going to do as soon as you talk to Leaky."

Leaky reached out to Hawk. Hawk took him by the hand, nearly sending him to his knees. Leaky had never been gripped by such a powerful man. "Glad to know you, Leaky."

"Same to you, Hawk."

"What can I do for you?" inquired Hawk, looking over Leaky's head and surveying the crowd.

"Thought you might have something for me to do. I'd kinda like to work my way out to the West Coast."

Hawk still looking beyond Leaky said, "Got all the help I need. Ward here was my last man."

"There," said Leaky, "I told you he wouldn't want an old

guy like me."

"What was that remark?" growled Hawk, glaring into Leaky's eyes.

"You heard me. No one wants anyone that's as old as me."

"I didn't say anything about your age, did I?" shouted Hawk, slamming his fists against his hips.

"No, but I know how it is."

"I brought Leaky here because I thought he might have something to offer," said Ward.

Hawk turned to Ward. "You're just like all the rest. Once you get a job you want to run everything."

"I'm sorry, Hawk, but Leaky is a mule skinner and a cook. I thought he might be able to relieve some of the women from time to time during some hard times. Who knows, maybe he could do some cooking for us."

"You sober?" asked Hawk, glaring at Leaky.

"Yes, I'm sober."

"You smell like a whiskey barrel and I don't allow no drinking on my trains."

"I did have a couple of drinks, but it weren't nothin'."

Hawk sized Leaky up. "Let me see your hands."

Leaky extended his hands. "What you want to see them for?"

Hawk stared for a moment. "You got some pretty good rein burns there, so I guess I can believe you when you claim to be a mule skinner."

"You calling me a liar?" snapped Leaky.

"No, I just said I can see the signs on a man's hands if he's been a mule skinner very long."

Ward watched Hawk's shifting eyes. A slight twitch came to Hawk's upper lip, when Ward said, "I think he would fit in, Hawk."

Hawk leaned forward and looked Leaky in the eye. "You in good health? I don't want to have to bury you on the way out."

Leaky bristled up. "They'll be burying you along the trail before they will me."

"All right, Leaky, you're on. But remember one thing, you had better carry your load or there will be hell to pay. I don't allow any freeloaders on my wagon train. You understand that?"

"You bet I do and you won't be sorry," declared Leaky, smiling from ear to ear.

Hawk reached for Leaky's hand. "Somehow I believe you."

Leaky grabbed his hat, danced around, then threw it high into the air. "I'm going to California, Ward, can you believe it?"

"Yes, Leaky I believe it."

"All right you two," shouted Hawk. "There's nothing for you to do down here, so be off with you. This ain't no circus and you standing around ain't going to help a damn bit."

Ward shrugged his shoulders, then tapped Leaky in the middle of his back. "I guess we're not wanted, so let's go on uptown."

"Sure sounds like a nasty fellow, don't know that I could stand him on a trip like this," replied Leaky, turning away and sauntering toward town with Ward.

"You must remember one thing, Leaky."

"And what's that?"

"You can't be a pussy cat and be a wagon master. It's a tough job and to be very frank with you, I don't know why anyone would want the job."

"I expect you're right, but how are all those women gonna take being ordered around all the time?"

"The women that are back there ready to risk life and limb are not the socialities you find back East. These women are made of different stuff."

"What do you mean?"

Ward stepping up on the boardwalk, continued on, "Today these women are being scoffed at by those tucked safely in their cottages back East. These women are as much the backbone to the West as are the men."

"I reckon you're right. I have a sister and I wouldn't want her heading out in one of these wagon trains."

Ward hesitated then went on. "I had a sister; she died of the influenza a couple of years back, never have gotten over that."

Having reached the saloon where Ward and Leaky first met, Leaky pushed aside the door and walked in ahead of Ward. It was nowhere near as crowded as it was when

Ward first went in. There were several places to stand at the bar.

The bartender glanced at Ward and then Leaky. "What happened to you, Leaky?"

"Nothing, why?"

"Nothing," exclaimed the bartender.

"Well, I did take a bath and got some of my hair cut off."

"I guess you did," smiled the bartender. "You look almost human."

Ward smiled and ordered a couple of whiskies while Leaky stood tapping his foot on the brass rail.

When the bartender returned with two glasses and a bottle of spirits, Leaky spoke up rather sharply, "Yes, I took a bath and you ain't gonna have to worry about me no more."

Directing his question at Ward the bartender spoke up, "What's he mean?"

"Let him tell you."

"All right, Leaky, what did you mean by that remark?"

"Just what I said. I have a job with one of the wagon trains leaving out of here in a couple of days."

"You're heading West?"

"That's right. I told you someday I would see the West for myself."

"I can't argue about that; you always did have that pipe dream."

Ward spoke up, "I don't know anything about Leaky's past, but he did sign on with a wagon train not more that an hour ago."

The bartender reached over the bar and shook hands with Leaky, "By damn, I never thought it would happen."

"To be honest with you, barkeep, if it hadn't been for Ward here, all I had to look forward to was being buried out there in that cemetery on the hill. That is if anyone would have bothered."

Following several drinks, Ward took Leaky to the boardinghouse where they rented a room and settled in for the night.

After Leaky had been in the room for a while he cautiously pulled back the blanket covering the bed he was suppose to sleep in. "Ward, I might just have to sleep on the floor tonight."

Ward scowled, "What are you talking about?"

"I haven't slept on sheets since I was a wee child."

"What does that have to do with sleeping on the floor?"

"I don't think I can sleep on a clean sheet."

"What are you talking about? You're clean, the sheets are clean, so you should sleep like a baby."

Leaky was still fussing while climbing into bed and covering himself up. "I'll try, but I don't think it is gonna work."

Ward laying with his hands locked behind his head, smiled when he heard deep breathing. Leaky was sound asleep.

✦✦✦✦✦✦✦CHAPTER THREE✦✦✦✦✦✦✦

THE FOLLOWING MORNING, Ward and Leaky made their way back to see Hawk down by the river where the wagon train was being assembled. Much to Ward's surprise the wagons were loaded and the teams were being hitched to them.

With an alarming tone in his voice Leaky asked, "They planning on leaving without us?"

"No," Ward assured him.

Moments later, Hawk's booming voice rang out. "Hey you two, get over here."

Ward looked around. Hawk was speaking to them. "What's up?"

Hawk's face was redder then ever. "We will be pulling out in about three hours."

"What can we do?" asked Ward.

"You see that lone wagon out there?" asked Hawk, pointing in a westerly direction.

"Sure do."

"Then you and Leaky get out there and hitch those two teams of mules up to it and wait for me there."

"What am I gonna do on this trip?" asked Leaky, rather forcefully.

Hawk whirled around and looked at Leaky. "You're going to be in charge of that wagon."

"You mean I'm going to drive those mules all the way to California?"

"You think you can do it?" inquired Hawk.

"Well, heck yes, I can do it."

"Then get out of here. I have more things to do than hold your hand."

Leaky started to sputter when Ward reached over and

took him by the shoulder. "Come on, Leaky. We've got things to do."

"He's treating me like a child," stammered Leaky, looking over his shoulder at Hawk who had already walked away.

"Hawk has a lot of responsibility here, Leaky, and I can assure you he's not going to put up with your whimpering."

"See, now you're treating me like a child."

"Then act like a man and you will be treated like a man."

Leaky puffed up like a toad, but said nothing. Instead, he fell in behind Ward who was still leading his sleek black stallion.

By the time Ward and Leaky had the teams hitched to the wagon, Hawk had the train assembled. It was the first time the settlers heard Hawk's powerful voice call out. "Move 'em out; we're heading for California!" From there Hawk rode out to where Ward and Leaky were standing. "Leaky, when the wagons go on by, fall in behind the last one and bring up the rear."

"Why can't I take the lead?" asked Leaky.

"Damn it," shouted Hawk, "because I said you're going to bring up the rear. Furthermore, if you give me any more lip, you'll stay here in Hannibal. Now, have you got that straight?"

Humbly, Leaky dropped his head. "Yes, sir, I do."

"Well," Hawk hesitated then looked to Ward, "I want you out on the point and if I see you're wandering, I'll let you know what direction to go."

"How far out should I go?"

"You want to be able to see the lead wagon and I sure want to be able to see you, so use that as your rule. If you see something you don't like, hold your rifle up and I'll stop the wagons and wait for you to go on ahead. No matter what happens, don't fire your gun unless you are in danger or the wagon train is in grave danger."

"I've got you." With that, Ward brought his horse around and headed west into a warm moist breeze."

Hawk turned to Leaky. "You see that horse tied to your wagon?"

"Sure do."

"That will be your horse, so treat him right. There isn't

another one for you if he goes down."

"I understand, Hawk."

By this time the first wagon was coming up on Hawk and Leaky. Leaky scowling said, "What's that woman doing driving those three teams?"

"That's Emily."

"So it's Emily, what's she doing driving those teams?" was Leaky's demanding outburst.

Hawk barked out at Leaky, "It's none of you damn business, but if you must know this is at least her tenth trip with me. She takes care of the women and acts more or less like a nurse."

"Never heard of such a thing," declared Leaky, brushing his beard with the back of his hand.

"Well, you've heard of it now and if you're just half the man as she is a woman, you and I will get along just fine." With that Hawk rode up alongside Emily's wagon. "You think you're ready for another long haul?"

"Sure am, Hawk, so let's move 'em out."

Hawk's smile was wide as he tipped his hat and gave Emily a wink. "Good luck, Emily."

She smiled back. "We'll make it all right."

Emily appeared to be in her mid-forties. A small woman with fine features. Leaky thought she should be in back of a desk teaching school instead of being in the lead wagon heading west. The wad of reins in each of her tiny hands turned her knuckles white as she took command of her teams and peered out from under a flowered bonnet. Leaky shook his head and waited for the train of thirty wagons to move on by, then fell in behind the last one.

The men of the train rode alongside their wagons armed with rifles and sidearms. It was a quiet time for most of them for they were heading into an unknown land with their women and children.

Hawk rode slowly along the train talking to men, women and children trying to assure them everything would be all right. However, with all of Hawk's confidence, fear and apprehension was on their faces. Hawk did not treat their fears lightly for he remembered only too well the first trip he made.

CHAPTER FOUR

THE WAGON TRAIN had rumbled over barren plains for weeks, then as dusk crept in on them one evening, large shadowed rock formations loomed up in front of them far to the west. Excitement ran rampant for it was the first time many of them had seen anything other than grassy or wooded mountain ranges. Hawk brought the train to a halt and motioned for Ward to come in off the point. Hawk's booming voice echoed as he called out for everyone to bring their wagons around and form the usual circle for the night.

"What did you see up there, Ward?" asked Hawk, watching the circle closing up on the far side.

"From where I was at, I saw what looked like a pass through that granite wall."

"There's one there, but we'll have to veer to the north in the morning in order to find it," said Hawk, motioning for Leaky to take his wagon inside the circle.

By this time everyone knew what to do. Families came together, pitching in and helping prepare a hot evening meal. Their evening meal was the only staple meal they had during the day.

After their meal, men came together and built a large fire in the center of the circle that would help ward off animals such as coyotes and wolves.

Hawk, Ward and two other men met by the fire to discuss the upcoming day. "Men," said Hawk, "this is the beginning of your trip to the West."

One of the men laughed out loud and was quickly put in his place by Hawk. "This ain't kids' play, Martin, and I wasn't joking when I said what I did. It's been a joy ride up until now, but from here on out the going gets tough."

Martin's face became stern. Hawk was the boss and he was going to get tougher as the going got tough. "Sorry, Hawk, didn't mean to make a joke out of anything."

"Then don't," barked Hawk. Hawk hesitated, then went on. "Now, what I have to tell you is not to go beyond this meeting, is that understood?"

They all shook their heads and listened intently to what he had to say. "It's rugged ahead and the going is damn hard on men, animals and equipment, but regardless of what happens we must go on. You're apt to see things happen here that you don't like, but I swear to God if any of you disobey my orders, I'll take you out with one shot from this trusty iron I have at my side. Is that clear?"

The men looked at each other then one by one they agreed.

Ward was the first one to speak up. "Are you going to tell us what to expect, Hawk?"

"First, the trail is wicked. Second, there are a couple of renegade bands of Indians in the territory and we can expect to run into them somewhere along the way. If they're not riled up about something, we can get by them without a fight, but if they are riled up we can expect a fight." Before saying anything further, Hawk shouted, "Leaky, where in the hell are you?"

"I'm right here, Hawk; what do you want?"

"As I told the others here, things could get tough the next couple of days, so you at the rear better keep your eyes pealed and don't let anything or anyone come up on us, is that understood?"

"Well—yes."

"You have something you want say, Leaky?" asked Hawk, pushing his hat to the back of his head.

"Nope, I know just what you want."

"How about the rest of you, is there anything bothering you that you want to talk about?" With nothing further, Hawk dismissed the men and headed for Emily's wagon.

Emily was outside preparing her meal when Hawk joined her. "What you got cookin'?"

"Been soaking sidepork, thought I would boil up a couple of pieces, would you like to join me?" asked Emily, glancing in Hawk's direction.

"I just might do that if you have enough for another mouth."

"I thought you would, so I put on a little extra."

After eating with Emily, Hawk stepped over a wagon tongue and walked outside the circle of wagons, seeing to it that the men guarding the camp were in position and alert. Satisfied with what he saw, he returned to the camp fire where he unrolled his bedroll and turned in for the night.

As the fire dimmed, calls from night creatures were all around them. Hawk hearing a wild call pushed himself up on one elbow and listened. It was as if a crow was calling somewhere in the darkness. Moments later an answering call came from some distance. A second call went out and it was answered from the opposite direction. Hawk crawled over to where Ward was asleep and woke him up.

"Yes, yes, what is it?"

Hawk with his mouth tight to Ward's ear said. "Get up slowly and bring your gun along. Wake up Leaky on your way by, but don't make any noise."

"But—"

"But, hell—do as I say."

With that, Hawk slipped quickly around the end of one of the wagons and disappeared into the darkness. Ward placed his hand over Leaky's mouth and whispered the same message to Leaky that Hawk had given him. Quietly the two men unnoticed, slipped away into the darkness. The night was black as pitch. Stopping, they waited until their eyes became adjusted to the darkness. While standing next to a wagon they saw a dark shadow. Ward whispered, "Is that you, Hawk?"

"Yes, but stay right there." Hawk went on by, but soon was back.

"What's the problem?" asked Ward, shifting his holster until if felt right on his hip.

"You hear those night birds?" asked Hawk quietly.

"I do," replied Leaky. "I been hearing them for some time now."

"So," said Ward.

Hawk came back strong. "So, what the hell do you mean by that?"

"Well, then what is it?"

"I'm guessing it's those renegade Indians I told you about."

"What's our next move?" inquired Ward.

"We don't do anything, but I do have the men on the outside alerted in case some braves try to enter our compound."

Leaky moved in close. "Do you think they'll try that?"

Hawk took a deep breath. "I don't believe so; I think they're just trying to set our teeth on edge. I'd say they will call all night and be out of here by morning."

"And if they don't?" asked Leaky, keeping a firm grip on his rifle.

"Then, we'll have to face whatever comes. The only thing we can do now is protect our livestock. Ward, you go back and throw all the wood you can find onto the fire; I want that fire roaring as soon as possible. In the meantime, I'll check the men on the outside."

"What about me?" asked Leaky, spitting his cud of tobacco out on the ground.

"Come with me," whispered Hawk. "And keep your distance."

Sparks filled the air as Ward threw wood on the fire. Flames leaped high in the night sky laying a perimeter of light far beyond the circled wagons. The livestock came into full view. It would not be hard to see someone approaching from out of the darkness.

Emily, a seasoned wagoner moved slowly from her wagon and approached Ward still throwing wood on the fire. "Are those pesky renegades out there again?"

Ward whirled around. Emily was facing his gun laying level to her heart. "Oh, Emily, it's you. I guess I'm a little jumpy at this point."

"Don't apologize, when this happened the first time I thought I was going die of fright."

Ward walked over to Emily, reached down and took her by the hands. "What makes you travel this route over and over?"

"Oh, I don't know. Maybe it's because I can be of some help by taking the personal problems of the travelers off Hawk's shoulders."

"I'm sure Hawk appreciates that. How many trips have you made with Hawk?"

"I don't rightly know, but there have been some hair raisers during that time."

"I expect there has, but laying all that aside, are you traveling to be with Hawk?"

Emily looked up, her face reddened from the cherry glow of the fire. "I should say that's personal, but I won't. I have never said this to anyone, but it's going to feel good to get it out...I love that man, can you understand that?"

"Can't say that I do, but only a woman can see what a man is really made of and I think you know that about Hawk."

"I sure do and he is a hell of a man. Do you realize that if it weren't for men like him the West would never be opened up?"

"I know that, Emily, and I'll keep your secret."

"Somehow I knew you would."

Just then Hawk stepped over a wagon tongue along with Leaky and headed toward Ward and Emily. "What you up for, Emily?"

"Do I have to tell you every time I leave the wagon and what I'm doing? Further—"

Emily was interrupted by an outcry from one of the men on the outside. Hawk whipped his iron out and fired it twice into the air. Men, women and children leaped from the wagons and came running toward the fire.

Hawk bellowed, "Everyone back to the wagons except you men. Now get yourselves armed and under the wagons. Don't fire unless I tell you to or unless one of them redskins is on top of you."

With that, Hawk and Ward left the circle and headed in the direction of the outcry. It was near the horses. On the ground laid Mr. Worton, dead and not a pretty sight.

The fire roared, making it as light as day, far beyond the circle of wagons. The cattle were spooked and the horses reared up, tugging at the ropes that tied them to the wagons. Ward ran frantically to where his horse was and untied him. His sleek black stallion had been under fire many times and sensed the danger in the night. Ward tied his horse to a nearby wagon tongue and joined Hawk who was looking down on Mr. Worton. "They'll pay for this, Ward. I'll kill one of them if I have to do it with my bare hands."

"You think they'll attack?" whispered Ward.

"I don't believe so. This bunch pulls sneak attacks. They have never been known to stand up and fight."

"But you don't really know do you?" asked Leaky, replacing his cud of tobacco with a new one.

"Hell no, I don't know. They are like wild animals out for the kill. They don't belong to a tribe, so they don't have a chief to account to. I still think they're from a tribe far north of here. But I'm telling you this, if I get my hands on one of them I'll skin him alive."

"Oh no, Hawk!" exclaimed Emily, looking longingly into Hawk's angry, but shadowed face.

"Don't tell me 'oh no,' I'm telling you."

Emily dropped her eyes. "Do you want me to go tell Mrs. Worton?"

Hawk swallowed hard. "Would you?"

Emily turned and headed for the Worton wagon. Her tiny frame was like a speck in the night. Hawk kicked at the dirt and sent sand like a cloud into the air. "You know, Ward, there goes one hell of a woman."

"I know, Hawk."

"What we gonna do with Mr. Worton?" chimed in Leaky, staring into the roaring fire.

Hawk flinched and rubbed his wiry beard. "We're going to have to bury him, but Mrs. Worton will have to be told first."

Emily had not been gone long when out of the night came the sound of a woman's voice shrieking and wailing. Mrs. Worton had been told of her husband's death.

"Sort of cuts your heart out, don't it?" sighed Leaky.

Hawk staring at the ground, shook his head. "I guess by damn it does and Emily is right in the middle of it. Don't know what I'd do if she ever said she wasn't coming with me, but on the other hand, why in the hell should she?"

Leaky shook his head. "I guess you'll have to answer that."

"Ward," said Hawk, "you and Leaky go out and drag Mr. Worton's body back and place it underneath that supply wagon over there."

Hawk waited until Ward and Leaky were out of sight and then joined Emily who sat outside the Worton wagon with Mrs. Worton's head in her lap. One of the other women was inside the wagon with the children, trying to console them.

Placing his hand on Mrs. Worton's shoulder, Hawk explained, "We will have to bury Mr. Worton; you know that don't you?"

Mrs. Worton sobbed her reply, "Yes, I know, but where?"

"We'll wait until we're ready to leave, then we'll bury him where we have the fire. I'll have some of the men cover the grave with ashes. The Indians shouldn't think to look for him there."

"Would they look for him?" whimpered Mrs. Worton, gazing up into Hawk's eyes that were filled with hatred.

"We don't know, but that's what we are going to do."

"Will someone say a few words over him? He was a good man, you know."

"I know he was and a good family man, I'll bet."

One of the other women from the next wagon was still with the two Worton children trying to console them.

"But who could say a few words?" asked Mrs. Worton.

"You know that Miss Flecher?"

"Yes."

"I often see her reading the Bible, so maybe her."

"Yes, I have also seen that. Would you ask her for me?" sobbed Mrs. Worton.

"Well—well—"

Emily, seeing Hawk was in over his head and floundering, spoke up, "I'll talk with her."

Mrs. Worton grabbed Emily by the hand. "Oh, thank you, thank you."

When Ward and Leaky returned, Hawk spoke softly, "The burial will take place in the morning."

"What can we do?" asked Ward.

"Nothing tonight," replied Hawk, shaking his head.

From there, Hawk selected a few hand picked men and placed them at key locations outside the circle of wagons, there to keep a keen eye open, making sure no one came out of the darkness and attack those on guard.

In the meantime, Emily found Miss Flecher consoling a

child who had been frightened by all of the commotion. "Miss Flecher, I must talk with you."

"What is it, Emily?"

"Where's the child's mother?" asked Emily, patting the small child on the head.

"I'm right here Emily; I'll take her into the wagon and see if I can calm her. Come along child." Still weeping, the little girl holding a china doll, followed her mother back to their wagon.

"Yes, Emily, what is it?" asked Miss Flecher, laying her Bible down and setting her glasses aside.

"Of course, you heard about Mr. Worton."

"Yes, what a dreadful thing; let's pray it's the last for this trip."

"We can only hope for that," replied Emily, sitting down beside Miss Flecher. "Now what I came to talk to you about is that we are going to bury Mr. Worton in the morning and we thought you might say a few words over him."

"Oh my, I don't know about that. I'm not a minister."

"There are a lot of things we are not by title, but we believe that with your faith it would be more than fitting for you to do this for all of us. I think we need it."

"I do appreciate your confidence, but how about Hawk?" asked Miss Flecher, glancing at Hawk's large frame standing guard in the center of the circle and near the roaring fire.

"It was he that suggested you."

"I feel honored and I guess it really becomes my duty to do this."

Emily gripped Miss Flecher's hand. "I was hoping you would say that and do try and get some rest."

Miss Flecher smiled and laid her head on Emily's shoulder for a moment. "You know you're a fine woman, Emily."

"I'm not as pure as I should be."

Miss Flecher took Emily by the hand. "In whose eyes?"

"Thank you, Miss Flecher, that was very thoughtful of you."

The two women parted. Miss Flecher returned to her wagon and Emily joined Hawk who was standing alert.

✥✥✥✥✥✥✥✥✥ CHAPTER FIVE ✥✥✥✥✥✥✥✥✥

THE REST OF THE NIGHT passed without incident. When daylight broke and the sun nestled below the eastern horizon, Hawk called for a muster in the center of camp. It was a ragged bunch that left their wagons and were assembled around what was left of the once roaring campfire. Children cried while rubbing their weary eyes. Women walked like the unknown and men cradled their weapons in their arms.

Hawk waited until every last one was accounted for and at the fire before speaking. "Ladies and gentlemen, we had a bad night and as I told you before we left Hannibal this could very well happen. All we can do is hope this will be the last, but I'm not going to tell you that and get your hopes up. I'm also not trying to frighten you. You're a tough lot or you wouldn't be here. I'm sure you had talked this out before you left and now that it has happened and we are at a point of no return. We're going to have to tighten our belts and go on. Is that understood?"

Hawk looked into their eyes and saw mixed emotions ranging from pure fright to numbness of the mind and body. "If so, you men clear the campfire area, for that's where we will conduct the burial of Mr. Worton. Rest his soul….You ladies don't need to be dressing up; we don't have time for that and Mr. Worton, if he were here would say, 'Let's get on our way West.'"

Much to Hawk's surprise, Mrs. Worton came forward, turned and addressed the crowd briefly. "Hawk is right. We were going West and that is what my husband would have said."

"You're a gracious lady, Mrs. Worton, and that's going to make it easier for all of us," said Hawk quietly.

Before the crowd broke up, one of the men from the back spoke up. "Do we need to fear anything during the day?"

Hawk growled, "We don't need to fear anything at anytime, but I would suggest we do."

The man nodded and returned to his wagon with his family. Their small child gripped his hand firmly.

Hot coals were dragged away and a shallow grave was dug. After they placed the body in the grave and covered it, Hawk said, "Ward, would you go see if Miss Flecher is ready?"

Ward nodded his head and walked over to Miss Flecher's wagon. "Are you ready, Miss Flecher?"

The front flap to the wagon opened and Miss Flecher appeared. "I expect I am as ready as I ever will be."

"Would you like me to walk with you over to the grave?"

"Would you?"

While walking with Miss Flecher to where Hawk was standing, Ward felt her slip her hand into his. He glanced down and found her looking up at him with soft blue eyes. "Are you all right, Miss Flecher?"

"As long as you hold my hand."

Slowly a crowd gathered. Emily had gone to the Worton wagon and returned with Mrs. Worton. Silence gripped the grim scene.

With Miss Flecher still holding onto Ward's hand, they approached the grave. Her hand slipped from his and she spoke with eloquence. After she had finished, nearly everyone rushed to her side. Each of them telling her what a fitting sermon she had given.

Mrs. Worton especially, with tear filled eyes spoke to her with a quivering voice. "You did a wonderful thing here today, Miss Flecher. And it will be with your words that I will carry on. I have the strength now and I know the children and I will see this trip through for my husband and their father."

"Thank you, Mrs. Worton, for your kind words."

"Bless you, Miss Flecher."

Miss Flecher turned away and took Ward by the hand. "Will you walk me back to my wagon?"

Ward smiled. "I would be glad to. And might I add you

did a fine job. No minister could have done better."
"But I felt so inferior, Mr. Taylor."
"Please call me Ward."
"Can you see why I feel this way?"
Ward stepped back and looked Miss Flecher in the eye. "No, I can't—"
"The name is Carman."
"May I call you Carman?"
She lifted her eyes. "I wish you would."
Ward looked into Carman's blue eyes. There was a sadness there, yet there was a twinkle. Her hair appeared to be wound into a bun on the top of her head and covered with a tight fitting bonnet, tied firmly under her chin. "All I can see is a fine young woman who did something seldom done by someone other than those of the cloth and she did a fine job."
"You're so kind, Ward, but I must get ready to travel." With that said, Carman pulled herself up into her wagon. Ward returned to the grave and helped cover it with ashes so as not to be detected by the renegades.
Emily, a loner, had everything ready for whenever Hawk called on them to move out. With time on her hands, she stayed at Mrs. Worton's side and helped her prepare to leave and to help her muster the strength she would need when she realized she would be leaving without her husband.
During this time, Emily kept a keen eye on Hawk for he had mounted his horse and was riding inside the circle of wagons, making one last check with everyone. Approaching the Worton wagon, Mrs. Worton ran screaming to meet him. "I can't leave, Hawk. I just can't leave him here alone."
Hawk swung himself off his horse and walked over to where Mrs. Worton was standing. Taking her in his powerful arms he hugged her and spoke softly. "Mrs. Worton, your husband wanted you out here or he would not have risk his family, isn't that right?"
"Yes, but we're no longer a family, Hawk."
"Please don't let your children hear you say that."
Mrs. Worton had soaked the front of Hawk's shirt before stepping back. "You're right. I can't let them think there is nothing left although I feel that way."

A warm and caring smile appeared out from under Hawk's large mustache. "You will make it, Mrs. Worton; you have the right stock in you to come out on top, believe me."

Mrs. Worton flashed a slight smile. "You think so?"

"I know you have, now I must go. And by the way, if you need anything just let Emily know, she'll get the word to me, is that understood?"

"Yes, Hawk."

Hawk nudged his horse in the ribs, who then galloped to the lead wagon. Ward had already rode out, scouted the nearby area and had just returned when Hawk rode up. "Anything unusual out there, Ward?"

"Nothing that I could see, but I did see what I thought was the turn north that you were telling me about yesterday."

"If you did it's just beyond those two huge rock formations to the left."

"That's the place."

"Did you ride through the pass?" asked Hawk, tightening his reins on his horse eager to go.

"For several hundred feet and I saw nothing."

"Did you see a large flat area beyond the rock?"

"That's where I turned back," replied Ward, reaching down and patting his horse on the neck.

Without warning, Hawk raised his voice, shouting, "Let's move 'em out."

Ward's horse reared up nearly sending Ward to the ground. After calming his stallion down, Ward strapped him on the rump and sped off to take the lead.

Leaky waited until the wagons had rolled on by, then dropped in behind them.

As the wagons rolled onward, a cloud of thick dust rose up and drifted to the east, leaving a marked trail in the air behind them.

Hawk's trained eyes swept every area they came upon. From time to time he rode the full length of the train checking on everyone, especially Mrs. Worton. She seemed to be holding up well, but she was nearly being torn apart like the rest, as they traveled over a rocky trail.

"Do you think these wagons are going to take this kind

of punishment?" shouted Mrs. Worton.

Hawk pulling up alongside said, "A lot of them have taken it and a lot of them as you'll see have been left along the trail."

"Do you think mine will take it?" called out Mrs. Worton, her voice shaking with every obstruction they lurched across.

"Ma'am," said Hawk, "if your wagon won't take this beating, every wagon in this train will be down and we'll walk to the big waters ahead."

"You're not just saying that, are you?"

"Mrs. Worton, we don't say things just to make people feel good out here; we tell it just the way it is."

"I respect you for that."

On the way by Emily's wagon, Hawk slowed, "How you coming, Emily?"

"Just fine, Hawk. How's Mrs. Worton doing back there?"

"A lot better than I thought she would. I thought we were going to have a real problem with her, but it's like I've said before, these people that are determined to go West are made up of the best stock in the country."

"I tend to agree with you, Hawk."

Hawk touched the brim of his hat, smiled at Emily and rode to the head of the train.

It was mid-afternoon when Hawk looked up and saw Ward riding hard toward him. Thundering to a stop, followed by a sand filled cloud of dust, Ward said quietly. "Hawk, there are Indians every place you look up there."

"Are there any on the ground that you can see?

"No, but they're high on the ledges above where we will be going."

"Then we don't need to worry. If the truth was known, the entire renegade band could be in sight. It's when you see only one or two high up, that should give us concern."

Ward went back to Leaky's wagon where he got himself a drink and started to leave.

"What's going on up there?" inquired Leaky, spitting in the wind.

"Nothing, I just wanted a drink."

"Come on, Ward. I'm not a child. What did you see?"

Ward cleared his throat, "If you don't say anything I'll

tell you."

"Good Lord, Ward, who would believe anything I said?"

"There are Indians all through the area ahead of us."

"So!"

"So, is that all you can say. Doesn't that worry you some?"

"Nope. When you get to be my age and you ain't worth anything to yourself or anyone else, what's there to worry about?"

"You sure don't think much of yourself, do you?"

"Yes, I do, but no one else does."

"I haven't got time to sit here and listen to you feel sorry for yourself."

"Well then, get yourself going."

With that, Ward spurred his horse, giving Hawk a wave on his way to the point.

It was sometime later when the wagon train turned north and was heading into the area where Ward had seen the Indians. Hawk sat high in his saddle and surveyed the territory. Leaky standing up in the wagon box craned his neck, trying to see the Indians Ward had told him about.

The day was tense for both Ward and Hawk. It was just before dusk that Hawk waved Ward in. "What's up?" asked Ward.

"We're going to veer to the right up here at the next pass; there's a large open field where we can camp. I'd like to go on, but I think we should make camp as soon as possible."

"Is there something you need to tell me?" asked Ward, looking at Hawk's deeply lined face.

"Damn if you can't ask more questions than anyone I've had along and to answer your question, there's nothing more I need to tell you."

Reaching a narrow opening in what appeared to be a solid wall, they moved their wagons through and out onto a wide open plain that stretched for miles.

"Why haven't we been traveling out here?" asked Ward.

"There you go again, asking questions."

"Well, damn it, I thought I was a part of this wagon train, not just someone that was traveling with it."

Hawk scowled and moved his jaw rather angrily. "You

are, Ward, but I ain't used to having someone out on the point that thinks for himself"

"I can't help that, but I can tell you one thing, if there's trouble brewing, my knowing it is going to help. Remember, I just got through fighting a war, so I do know something about keeping alive."

"I know you do and no doubt we can learn from each other."

"I was thinking about something. I sure don't know how you handle things out here, but between the two of us, I think we can be one tough team."

Hawk looked up at Ward, then extended his hand. "You're right. I guess it's because you look so young that makes me think you're not responsible."

Emily had just walked up behind Hawk. "That's not true."

Hawk whirled around. "What are you doing out here, Emily?"

"I just smelled trouble and wondered what you two were planning for us. Yes, and didn't we pull off the trail like this once before?"

"Yes, Emily, we did, but we don't need to be talking about that."

"It's like this, Ward," said Emily. "Hawk just doesn't like to have someone along that's as smart as he is, now that sums it all up."

Hawk looked harshly at Emily then smiled. "Shucks, Emily, that's not true and you know it."

"Well, maybe not, but it seems you can't take it when someone has a better idea than you do."

Ward smiled to himself and turned his head. Emily was reading Hawk like a book and Hawk knew it.

Hawk without replying to Emily, strapped his horse on the rump and began shouting for everyone to form a circle for the night.

Emily watched Hawk take control and looked up at Ward. "Please don't put him down too much, will you? He really is a nice fellow."

"Oh, Emily, I like the man and respect him. I can't think of anyone I would rather be on this trip with than Hawk."

"Thanks, Ward," said Emily, turning and walking toward

her wagon.

The circle was formed and the men were piling wood in the center of the compound readying it for a fire. Hawk made a point of stopping at each wagon and talking to everyone. Ward still on his horse sat bewildered, for Hawk did not mingle with many of the people traveling with him.

When Hawk rejoined Ward, he turned and shouted at the top of his voice, "Hit the dirt!" The force could have shaken boulders hanging loose in the mountain range to the rear. From the wagons, men scrambled with rifles in their hands. Once out they threw themselves onto the ground and crawled under their wagons with their rifles firmly against their shoulders.

Ward pulled his side arm and readied it. "What's going on?" he asked Hawk anxiously.

"I'm looking for trouble and I want everyone to be ready for anything that comes our way—" Before Hawk could finish, he looked to his right and there under her wagon was Emily, shouldering a gun nearly as large as she was.

"Would you look at that, Ward."

"I see her. She sure is one hell of a woman," commented Ward. A slight smile graced his face.

"No sense of saying anything to her or she'll be all over me."

"I'll bet," remarked Ward.

"That was a good job, men, but keep close to the wagon wheels. They're not much protection, but they are some.... All right you can go on about your way, but remember I want the children kept inside the wagons while we're camped here."

Shortly after the fire was lit one of the men standing guard on the outside shouted, "The Indians are coming!"

Hawk looked up. A band of screaming Indians, riding hard, were coming down out of the mountainous area heading for the compound. Hawk shouted at the top of his voice and fired one shot in the air. Men scrambled to the ground and clawed their way under the wagons. Not a shot was fired. Hawk had told them to hold their fire until he fired his rifle a second time.

They were coming on fast and Emily lay directly in front of the first wave of screaming braves. It appeared to

Ward that Hawk had waited until they had come dangerously close before firing. Smoke rolled out from under the wagons and the air was filled with slugs. Ward saw two of the Indians leave their horses and drop to the ground dead. The Indians circled the wagons, firing at random.

Suddenly, Ward shouted to Hawk. Hawk spun around and was looking into the eyes of a mounted Indian who had breached the circle. Hawk gritted his teeth and fired; the young brave fell from his horse and dropped to the ground.

"How many more we got coming?" shouted Ward, dropping his gun to his side while watching the Indians retreat into the foothills.

Hawk wiped his brow. "I didn't think there were that many out there."

"Is this still the renegade band?" shouted Ward.

Hawk ignored Ward. "Hold your fire, men. No sense throwing lead in the air." Hawk paused, "Anyone hit?"

With no reply to his question, Hawk spoke loud and clear, "Stay right where you are, men; they'll be back."

Ward, still mounted, rode outside the circle then struck out in the same direction the Indians had come from.

"Hold up there, Ward," yelled Hawk, shaking his fist in the air.

Ward's black steed ran like the wind and soon they were out of sight.

Hawk slammed his foot into the ground and made one long kick in the air. "Damn kid is going to get himself killed riding off like that."

"That's just what you would have done when you were his age, Hawk." It was Emily, who had left her position and was standing behind him.

"What are you doing out here? I thought I told everyone to stay where they were."

"I thought that was for those other folks, not me."

"Damn it, Emily, if the others see you going against my word it will give them cause to try the same thing."

"You don't have anything to worry about. Don't you think these people know there is something between you and I?"

"Have you said anything?"

"Well, of course not, but they're all of average intelligence."

Hawk was still staring intently at the spot where Ward had disappeared. He wiped his mustache and pushed his hat to the back of his head.

"It's not going to help, you standing there worrying him back, Hawk," said Emily.

"I know it, but he's one fine young man and I don't want anything to happen to him. If I'd known what he was going to do, I would have gone out with him."

"You do have a soft heart, Hawk," smiled Emily, pulling at a loose cord hanging from his sleeve.

It wasn't long before the sound of thundering hooves roared and a cloud of dust rose up from behind the sloping hills to the north. Hawk dropped to his knees and put his ear to the ground. "It's a herd of buffalo on the move."

"They coming our way?" inquired Emily anxiously.

"Don't rightly know, but by the looks of that cloud of dust they're heading east."

Back on his feet, Hawk strained his eyes far to the west. "Emily, is that Ward on his way back?"

Emily stepped in between a couple of wagons and looked out. "Yes, that's him and look at him come."

"Is he being followed?" asked Hawk.

"It doesn't look like it."

Soon Ward rode up and stopped within the circle where he jumped to the ground.

Hawk bristled up and stormed over to where Ward was standing with his alert steed. "Why did you go and do a thing like that?"

"I wanted to see how many there were."

"Well, did you find out?"

"They just disappeared without a trace."

"Did you expect they would be out there just waiting to welcome you into their camp?" growled Hawk, shaking his jaw like a mad dog.

"Now Hawk," said Emily softly, "let it drop. He was doing what he thought you had hired him for."

A bit surly, Hawk said rather sharply, "Get back to your station, Emily; I'll run this wagon train anyway I want to, do you hear me?"

Emily smiled. "Aren't you forgetting who you are talking to, Hawk?"

"Nope, I know what I'm doing," Hawk stuttered some. "Please Emily, be careful. I don't know what I would do without you."

"I will be, Hawk, I promise, but I'll tell you one thing, if they want a good fight, they've come to the right place."

"I like your spunk, Emily," whispered Hawk.

A half hour had passed during which time Hawk was like tension on a bow. Then from the west coming toward the encampment roared the thundering band of renegades. War cries filled the air. "All right, men, they mean business this time, but don't fire until I do. I'll try to take out their leader. Make every shot count; they have more reserve than we do."

They saw the paint on the braves faces before Hawk's powerful rifle roared, sending the lead Indian to the ground. Several Indians breached the compound and rode on through, but not before they torched two of the wagons. Women and children leaped to the ground and joined their husbands and fathers under the wagons. Rifles cracked, choking clouds of gun smoke cut at the back of their throats. Children cried and mothers huddled with their bodies over their quivering children. The Indians moving in a circle around the wagon fired point blank at the settlers defending all they owned.

"Get down, Ward! When they come around the next time they'll breach our defenses again," shouted Hawk.

Ward threw himself to the ground and crawled behind a nearby horse that had fallen from gunfire.

With blazing guns, the renegades charged the settlers once more and overran their position in several places. Hawk had been winged, but was standing his ground firing his two handguns recklessly.

Suddenly, Ward ran to Hawk's side and pointed north while shouting, "We'll never make it, Hawk."

Over the rolling hills to the north rode what seemed like hundreds of Indians, bearing down on Hawk's stubborn group.

Hawk looked up. Throwing his rifle into the air, he shouted at the top of his voice, "Broken Arrow, what a sight to see!"

The renegade band rode off and soon was out of sight behind the rocky foothills.

"What do we do now?" called out Ward.

"Hold your fire, men," yelled Hawk. "Hold your fire; these Indians are coming to help."

Not one man, woman or child left their positions under the wagons. Instead, they kept the Indians riding toward them in their sights.

"Come on, Ward," said Hawk, taking Ward by the arm. "We have friends to welcome."

"We have friends out here?" exclaimed Ward.

"Yes, friends," replied Hawk, stepping over a wagon tongue and heading out to meet Chief Broken Arrow. The chief had left his braves several yards back and was riding slowly toward Hawk.

With their right hands raised in a gesture of peace, both men nodded.

"They are angry young men, Hawk. The white men raided a small tribe of Yokees just north of here, killing old men, women and children."

"Is that why these young braves have left their tribes and become renegades, Chief Broken Arrow?"

"That is right. They trust no white man. If it had not been you, Hawk, I would not have brought my braves to save this wagon train."

"That's why we are friends, chief."

"Yes, Hawk. Trust is like the sun and the moon—it is unwavering."

"Are your men angry at us?" asked Hawk.

"No, white friend, they all know you and trust you."

Emily had crawled out from under the wagon and was bursting with pride to see Hawk speaking to Chief Broken Arrow.

"I want to thank you, Chief Broken Arrow, but I think we can handle it from here," said Hawk.

The chief raised his hand, "No, Hawk, we will camp nearby and in the morning we will see you through the land controlled by these young braves with revenge in their hearts."

"Will these renegades attack your village while you are gone?"

"No, Hawk, I have sent the word out that if they harm any one of my people we will be tying feathers on our spears with their hide."

"You are not a violent man, chief."

"Violence has nothing to do with it. It is up to me to protect my people in what ever manner I see fit."

"You are right, Chief Broken Arrow. I have that same responsibility."

"We are much alike, Hawk." With that Chief Broken Arrow raised his hand, turned his horse and rode back to where his braves were waiting.

"You know him well, don't you?" asked Ward, going out to meet Hawk.

"Yes, we have been friends for a long time and I'm damn glad he was in the territory or that band would have wiped us out before they were done."

"You think so?" asked Ward, striding back to camp with Hawk.

"I know so; they've got blood in their eyes for any white man and believe me if some cavalry unit slaughtered off old men, women and children, these braves, out of control, will kill every white man they lay their eyes on."

Once in the center of the circle of wagons, Hawk shouted out a message to everyone. "It's all right to come out from under the wagons; we have nothing to fear tonight. Go on about your way and feel safe for as long as Chief Broken Arrow and his braves are out there we have nothing to worry about."

"But they're also savages, Hawk," called out a man just getting to his feet.

"I don't give a damn what you want to call them. Chief Broken Arrow keeps his word more than those running the operation for the military out here."

The man slurred his voice slowly, "I just don't know."

"Well, I do and if you want to sit around worrying all night, I guess that's up to you." Hawk reached down and picked up his rifle that was laying on the ground and walked over to where Emily was standing.

"I'm so darn proud of you, Hawkshaw," said Emily. "There ain't another man in this whole world with the courage to go out and face those hundreds of Indians."

"He's my friend, Emily."

"If the cavalry should ride into his camp while he is gone and kill off some of his people, do you think he would still be your friend?"

"You're damn right he would be."

Emily glared at Hawk. "You can be a good friend of your dog, but just don't try and take his bone away from him."

Joining into the conversation, Ward asked, "By the way, Hawk, how did you and the chief become friends?"

"It's a long story and besides that I never have told anyone, so don't ask again."

After Hawk had started making his rounds of the wagons, Ward asked Emily, "How did they become friends?"

"You're not going to believe this, but I swear I'm telling the truth when I say, I don't know."

"Really?"

"That's right, Ward. I could never get it out of him."

✛✛✛✛✛✛✛✛✛CHAPTER SIX✛✛✛✛✛✛✛✛✛

A FIRE WAS BURNING in the center of the compound and each of the settlers were with their family. Many of them were not eating that night; the encounter with the Indians had left them unnerved and full of fear. Hawk was convincing about Chief Broken Arrow being his friend, but still mistrust lurked in the minds of many.

Ward made his way over to Carman's wagon and found her sitting outside. "Good evening, Carman."

"Good evening, Ward, and how are you?"

"I guess I have shook off the raid of this afternoon."

"My, that was something wasn't it? How does Hawk know who his friends are? I can't tell the difference."

"Hawk is a very wise man. Doubt if he could get along very well east of the Mississippi, but he sure knows what he's doing out here all right."

"I must say, I'm glad I found my way into his train instead of one of the others," commented Carman.

"All the men heading up these trains are good men, but I do agree, I'm glad I'm with Hawk."

Carman had laid a blanket down and was sitting in the center of it.

"Do you mind if I sit down here with you. I've been in the saddle or on my feet for hours," sighed Ward, dropping to his knees and then sitting on the blanket next to Carman.

"I guess you're down already, aren't you?"

"I'm sorry. If you don't want me here, I'll move on."

"No, no, Ward. I didn't mean anything like that; you're more than welcome. It will be good to have someone to talk with."

After nearly an hour, a large white moon appeared over the horizon lighting up the night. Indian campfires dotted the hillside around the encampment. Young braves were alert and watching over the wagon train. Occasional bird-like calls from the renegades were heard, but there were no answers.

It was mid-evening and people were strolling around the encampment, relaxing before turning in for the night. The moon, now nearly overhead, shown its bright light down on a quiet, but tense scene. Glances between Carman and Ward were warm. He reached over and placed his hand on hers. "Do you mind?"

"No, I rather like it."

Carman's eyes twinkled like starlight reflecting from the heavens as she squeezed Ward's hand and looked into his smiling face. Ward moved closer to her and as he did, Carman reached for her bonnet, pushed it back and off her head. She gently shook her long dark hair out, letting it come to rest about her shoulders. Removing her spectacles, she placed her palms behind her and leaned back. "My, the moon is beautiful."

"Yes," agreed Ward, "and so are you, Carman."

"Would you call me Carman when we are alone?"

Ward smiled and gazed into her eyes. "Yes, Carman, I will and that name just seems to fit you."

"How's that?"

"Oh, I don't know. I guess you look like a Carman."

"I think I like that," she responded, squeezing Ward's hand once more.

Ward, spellbound with Carman's beauty, stumbled when speaking to her. "You...you look different. Your hair is glistening in the moonlight and your eyes sparkle like stars that have been dropped from the heavens, nestling in them."

"You make me feel like a woman, Ward."

"Is that what you want to feel like?"

"Oh, yes, more than anything in the whole world."

"May I ask you something?" asked Ward, leaning forward and stroking Carman's hair, then touching her lips with his finger.

"Yes, what is it?"

"Have you ever been in love?"

"No. Have you?"

Ward moved closer and placed his lips to hers, Carman sighed and dropped her head back between her shoulders. "That was wonderful, Ward, but I think we should stop here."

"I think you're right." Ward got to his feet, reached down and helped her up. As their bodies came together Ward placed his arms around her and kissed her warm moist lips. "See you in the morning?"

"Yes, Ward."

"Are you going to wear your hair down?" he asked.

"If you'd like."

"Yes, please do, you're so much a woman this way."

"Wasn't I before?" Quickly she placed her finger on Ward's lips. "That wasn't fair and I was only joking with you."

Ward smiled and said, "Good night, Carman," as he stepped off toward the roaring fire in the center of the compound.

CHAPTER SEVEN

MORNING ARRIVED to the snapping of canvas flaps. A stiff wind was blowing in from the West. While the settlers were tying everything down on their wagons, Hawk and Ward rode out to where Chief Broken Arrow and his braves were waiting.

With his right hand raised, Hawk said, "It's not necessary that you come with us, Chief Broken Arrow."

"I feel it is. It will be some time before this band of angry braves forgets what happened two day lights ago."

"We'll be moving out soon, Chief Broken Arrow," said Hawk, tugging on his horse's reins.

A nod from Chief Broken Arrow sent Hawk back to prepare to leave.

With Ward at his side, Hawk returned to camp. "All right everyone, we're moving out; if you're not ready, say so." There was no reply. Hawk raised his arm and motioned the lead wagon to go forward. "There's nothing to fear, so move 'em out."

Mules, horses and oxen leaned into their tugs. Wagons creaked. A wild wind drove sand into the faces of both animals and men. Before leaving, the front flaps of each wagon were tied shut, yet the sand found its way inside. Children and those on the ground walking carried their hands in front of their faces and walked with their heads down to avoid the stinging sand.

Ward rode on ahead, flanked by a column of Indians on each side. Once in among the jagged rock formations towering high in the air, the sand no longer cut at their faces; instead it sifted down and built up on every surface.

Hawk with an eye on Ward, saw him turn north and disappear. The accompanying Indians rode nearby. Time passed slowly before Ward turned onto a trail heading west. The wagon train moved on through the sand storm that morning and when the storm subsided in mid-afternoon, Chief Broken Arrow approached Hawk.

"What is it, Chief Broken Arrow?"

"We will be with you until we reach the next fork. We will camp in the pass over night. This will give you the distance you will need to be safe from the hostile braves."

"Thank you, brother. I'll bring you something from the East my next trip through."

Chief Broken Arrow raised his hand in peace then brought his hand across his chest.

Hawk too crossed himself then rode to the front of the wagon train.

At the next pass some hours away, Chief Broken Arrow and his braves came to a halt and let the wagons pass between their two columns. Then like a whiff of dust, the Indians disappeared into the pass and were gone.

Moving over rocky terrain, men and equipment took untold punishment with every foot of ground they covered. Horses floundered and many had to be unharnessed before they could get to their feet. It was impossible for the settlers to stay in their lurching wagons. Those driving the teams walked alongside, followed by women and children. Ahead as far as the eye could see were even larger formations and beyond that were large gray walls of granite. Mountains that had been tossed from the bowels of the earth were reaching for the heavens.

Carman, with longing eyes, looked to the west for a glimpse of Ward, guided her two teams of horses that had pulled her wagon from Hannibal. With her bonnet tied tightly under her chin she again appeared to be a studious woman, unaware of the world around her. That, however, was not the case. Her mind was wise and courage ran through her veins.

Emily, stubborn as a mule and wise as a fox, walked beside her teams, dodging the hazards along the way.

It was late afternoon when a call came out to hold up. A wagon near the rear of the column had lost a wheel and overturned. The wagon tongue moving like a giant club knocked the teams of mules to the ground. Men with brute strength worked to free the animals.

"Cut the tugs," cried out one of the men, "or this one is going to break a leg before we can free him."

In danger of being kicked to death, men worked frantically through flying hooves to cut the teams loose. One by one the mules were brought to their feet and led away.

"Cut that water barrel off that wagon," shouted Hawk. "We can't waste the water."

Slowly the spinning wagon wheels stopped. It was the right rear axle that had given way.

"Are the mules all right?" called out Hawk.

The man holding the animals shook his head yes.

"Good," replied Hawk. "We might need an extra team to get these wagons through tomorrows leg of our journey."

"What about my belongings? We can't leave them here," exclaimed Herman Spade, owner of the overturned wagon.

Hawk walked over to where Spade was standing near the disabled wagon and placed his hand on the man's shoulder. "Do you have a spare rear axle?"

"Well, of course not."

"Then what would you suggest we do with all of your belongings."

Spade dropped his eyes. "I'm ruined."

Hawk's face reddened. "You're still alive aren't you?"

"Well, yes."

"You're family has gone unhurt, haven't they?"

Still staring at the ground, Spade replied, "Yes."

"Then what the hell are you complaining about?"

Emily hearing what was going on joined in the conversation. "I can take some of your things in my wagon."

"So can I," added Carman.

Mrs. Worton, with her skirt held high, hurried over to where the wagon lay on its top. "I can throw out most of my husband's things. This will make room for your children to ride and sleep."

Leaky who had been standing alongside Emily said, "I think I can take on everything you really need and your wife can sleep in the wagon."

"There," snarled Hawk. "Now do you think you can figure out the rest?"

"Yes, but there are things in there that are treasured by

my wife. We can't leave them here."

"Then you can stay here with them, we just don't have any more room," barked Hawk.

"Herman," said Spade's wife, "Hawk is right about everything. What is important is that we are together as a family."

"But what about the picture of your mother and father you cherish so much?"

"Herman, I'll keep mother and father in my heart until I die; is that clear to you? Now let's unload what we need and get it into the wagons of these wonderful friends. We still have a long journey ahead of us."

"Thank you, ma'am," said Hawk, touching the brim of his hat.

Returning to where Ward was on lookout, Hawk said, "I'm sure glad every man with us is not like that Spade fellow, or we wouldn't be out of Hannibal yet."

"Wouldn't you say, all in all these are a fine bunch of people?" added Ward.

"You bet they are. One of the best I've had in a long time, so I guess I should just stop complaining."

"How much delay is this going to cause?" asked Ward.

"We'll be out of here in a half hour, that is if they can get Spade out of the way."

"What do you think we got, a couple of hours to travel?" asked Ward, looking toward the west.

"At least. I'd like to get as many miles between us and those renegades as possible."

"I sure understand that."

It wasn't long before Leaky approached Hawk. "I guess we're ready to roll. That Spade fellow is still upset, but the rest of his family is doing all right."

"Are the two teams ready to go?"

"Oh, yes. I'm just glad they were mules instead of horses," said Leaky, wiping the tobacco juice off his whiskers.

"You're right," agreed Hawk. "A mule sure has a place in this world."

Hawk mounted his horse and rode slowly along the wagons asking if there were any reasons for not moving on. Reaching the Spade family, Spade puffed up as if he had something he wanted to say. However, before one word was said, Hawk leaned forward and stuck his finger in Spade's face. "Now you listen to me, Spade, I know this was a hell of a thing to happen, but I want to tell you there will be more hard times fall upon us before we get to our destination. I don't know where, or how or to whom it will fall on, but it will happen. Do you hear me?"

Spade took a deep breath. Hawk leaped to the ground and grabbed Spade by the front of his shirt. "Spade, I'm about to mop the ground with you if you don't shut your damn mouth and stop whimpering about your misfortune."

Spade's eyes were as large as saucers. "I hear you, Hawk, and I can assure you, you have heard the last of this from me."

"That's better, Spade, now we understand each other." Hawk patted Spade on the back, smiled at Spade's wife, then mounted his horse and returned to the head of the train.

Ward spurred his horse and rode on ahead. Hawk turned in his saddle and bellowed, "All right, let's move 'em out!"

It was nearly an hour when Hawk looked up and saw Ward sitting on his horse with his hands resting on his saddle horn.

"What's up?" asked Hawk.

"Don't know, but as I came into a grassy plain ahead I thought I could smell smoke."

Hawk scowled. "There's not a wagon train within two hundred miles of here; can't imagine what it could be."

"You believe me, don't you?" asked Ward.

"Well, yes, I believe you, but let's not alarm the rest."

"Should we be alarmed?" inquired Ward, shifting himself in his saddle and looking Hawk directly in the eyes.

"I don't think so."

"You don't think so," repeated Ward. "Then what are you thinking about?"

By this time the wagons had caught up with Hawk and Ward.

"I'll go back out," said Ward, raising his reins.

"Ward."

"Yes, Hawk."

"Don't go beyond the point you smelled the smoke, do you hear me?"

"Well, yes—"

"Did you hear me, Ward?"

"I'll be waiting for you at the end of the pass."

Ward reaching the point where he would meet up with the wagons, sat staring beyond the open valley. Mountains reaching into the clouds and as far as he could see south and north and beyond. Snow capped peaks loomed up and reflected the sun not yet setting, but hovering over distant lands. Ward had never seen the likes of them although he had heard of the rocky barrier that lay between east and west. The war had taken him into the mountains of the south and compared to what he could see, they were small in every dimension.

A soft cool breeze came up and was blowing in from the north. Ward sensed the smell of smoke riding in on the breeze once more. Standing high in his stirrups he tried to locate some sign of smoke. He scanned the northern horizon and saw nothing. Yet, the smell was stronger than before. While still searching the horizon, he was brought back to reality by the sounds of the wagon train approaching through the last section of the narrow pass.

Turning in his saddle, the first team of oxen appeared, being fronted by a young lad of fourteen or such. Ward watching the young boy, could not help but wonder where the lad's childhood had gone. It was no wonder that many of the men as they were referred to in the West were seventeen and eighteen years of age. Being reared by a father and mother that were willing to sacrifice everything they owned as well as themselves and their family, it was no wonder they were men and women by the time they reached their teens.

Whirling his horse around, Ward rode back to where Hawk was astride his horse at a critical bend, rounding a jagged rock formation. Ward waited until the last wagon cleared the area before speaking to Hawk.

"That's a tight one, isn't it?"

"Sure is, but we have a bunch a damn good teams here. Best I have ever seen."

"That's a load off your mind," said Ward, wiping his brow with his sleeve.

"You don't really know until you travel with some of

these men who never drove anything other than a horse and buggy."

"I never would have thought of that," commented Ward, removing his hat and brushing his hair off his forehead. "For that matter, there's been a lot of things happen here that I never thought of before."

Hawk smiled. "It seems like I learn something new every time I come out here. If it's not the elements, it's the people that make up the train."

Ward grinned, "You can have your job, Hawk; I think I'll be a banker."

Hawk for the first time in Ward's presence, roared with laughter. "Let's go see what it looks like out there on the plains. These mountains give me a feeling of being closed in."

Ward took up the slack in his reins and then said, "Where's Leaky? I don't remember him going by."

Hawk sat up straight in his saddle. "I don't think I did either, so hold up the train.

Ward pulled up to the last wagon and driver. "Pass the word up the line to stop the wagons, we're going back to see if we can locate Leaky."

Ward and Hawk rode hard back down the trail in search of Leaky. Hawk was blazing mad that no one in the train had been watching out for Leaky. It was several miles back that they spotted his wagon. Approaching they found him straddling a mule's hind leg.

"What's the problem, Leaky?" called out Hawk.

Leaky looked up. Sweat was pouring down his weather-beaten face. "He's got a sharp piece of stone buried in his foot right near the frog."

"Can I give you a hand?" asked Ward, dropping to the ground.

"Don't believe so; I think I got it coming right now." Leaky gritted his teeth while the mule jerked his leg. Leaky held on while the mule kicked wildly at the wagon box with the other foot.

"Hang on, Leaky," said Hawk.

"What the hell do you think I'm doing?"

Ward chuckled.

"Laugh you dumb dumbs, but if this animal doesn't stop

kicking, the buzzards will have something to eat on for a long time."

Hawk turned away to keep from laughing in Leaky's face.

"There," panted Leaky, letting go of the mule's leg and jumping as far away from the beast as possible. The mule, still harnessed, kicked at the wiffletree and slammed his hooves into the wagon box.

"Is all of this because it felt good to get that piece of rock out of his foot?" asked Ward.

Leaky, leaning against a large boulder and wiping his brow, yelled, "Hell no, he's just mad at me and the whole world right now."

"When you going to be able to drive him?" asked Hawk.

"He'll settle down as soon as he gets tired of kicking everything in sight, and that would be me if I got near him."

"He doesn't seem to be bothering his teammate," commented Ward, walking over to where Leaky was standing.

"No, she's just like most women. She watches this young stud get all mad and she just stands there and lets him carry on."

After waiting a few minutes, Leaky climbed up on the wagon and took the reins firmly in his hands. Rolling the reins out over the team's back he said, "All right you two, let's hit the leather." The mules stretched into their collars and moved forward. Leaky looking at both Ward and Hawk, shrugged his shoulders. "You see, he's already forgotten it."

Hawk rode on ahead while Ward stayed with Leaky until he reached the train. By that time Hawk was busy watching the settlers form a circle of wagons for the night.

Ward still concerned about the smell of smoke, spoke to Hawk about it again. "I'm going to ride on out and see if there's another encampment of settlers out there or if we are sitting in Indian territory."

"Suit yourself, but don't be gone long and don't be taking any chances."

Ward was about to leave when he heard someone say, "You're not going to ride out there, are you?"

Ward looked around. It was Carman standing near him.

"Why, yes."

"I hate to see you ride out there alone," exclaimed Carman, picking at her fingers.

"What's the difference? I'm out there all day anyway."

"I didn't say I liked that either, so I want to ride out on the point with you tomorrow."

Hawk spoke up, "That's no place for a woman, and you are a woman, ma'am."

Carman removed her bonnet and spectacles and tossed her head. Her dark hair dropped over her shoulders and down her back. Hawk's eyes blazed with wonderment.

"Well, I never saw a woman transform herself from one person to another as you've just done."

"Is that good?" asked Carman, smiling up at Hawk.

"Well, of course, ma'am, you are a very beautiful woman."

"Thank you, Hawk," Carman hesitated briefly. "May I go with you, Ward?"

Ward looked at Hawk. Hawk shrugged his shoulders. "It's up to you."

"All right," said Ward. "But if things get hot out there, you must ride as fast as you can back to camp."

"Can't promise you that; now I'll go get my horse."

"Did you ever see anything like that?" asked Hawk, shaking his head. "I thought she was just exactly what she looked like."

Moments later, Carman rode up and was ready to head out with Ward.

"Now you two had not better be taking any chances. Ward, you told Carman if things get hot out there she was to come on back, well that goes for you, too. Do you hear me?"

"I hear you," replied Ward, smiling at Carman.

"Did you pay any attention to me?" shouted Hawk, glaring at Ward.

"Yes, Hawk, I heard you and we'll be cautious."

"Yes, cautious, that's the word I wanted."

Ward spurred his horse as did Carman and they thundered off toward the north. It was from that direction that Ward thought he smelled the smoke.

Hawk in the meantime, shook his head and muttered to

himself, "Women can ruin a good man and the way Ward looks at her, I hope he doesn't lose his head over her."

"And what would be wrong with that?"

Hawk whirled around and standing almost in his hip pocket was Emily. "What's wrong with what?"

"What's wrong with Ward losing his head over Carman? She seems to be a very nice girl."

"I didn't say she wasn't a nice girl, did I?"

"Maybe not in so many words, but you were thinking about it."

"I was not and you know it."

Emily looked up at Hawk. "If you want to get your mind off of Carman and how beautiful she is, you can always remember what I looked like years ago."

"Emily, you still are the most beautiful woman in the world."

"I'm getting at little wrinkled, Hawk."

"Well, I ain't no kid no more myself."

"I know, but you're just as handsome as the day I first laid my eyes on you, Hawk. What a man, muscles and a full head of hair. Twinkling eyes that could send any woman mooning over you. And just think, I'm the one that follows you back and forth over this Godforsaken land."

"You don't have to come, Emily."

Emily looked deep into Hawk's squinting eyes. "Yes, I do, Hawk and you know it."

"Shucks, Emily, you know how I feel about you."

"Yes, I know."

Hawk threw his shoulders back. "What did you mean when you said I used to have a full head of hair. What do you think I have now?"

"I wouldn't know, Hawk, you don't even take your hat off when we are close, so very close." With that, Emily turned and walked away.

Hawk swallowed hard and removed his hat. "You see, Emily, I do have hair."

Emily looking back, replied, "Why don't you show me when we're alone?"

✦✦✦✦✦✦✦✦CHAPTER EIGHT✦✦✦✦✦✦✦✦

IN THE MEANTIME, Ward and Carman were out of sight and riding north. It was an area of brown grass and rolling hills. The further they rode into the unknown, the stronger the smell of smoke became.

"I can sure smell the smoke you were talking about, but I can't see where it's coming from," commented Carman, standing in her stirrups.

"We're close to something," Ward paused. "Let's dismount and walk to the crest of that hill straight ahead."

Carman and her horse fell in behind Ward, as they walked cautiously to the top of the hill.

"Oh, my Lord," exclaimed Carman. "Would you look at that."

Ward stopped short and gasped after surveying the ugly scene that lay before him. It was a burned out Indian encampment. Vultures soared overhead while others worked viciously at the campsite. Burned out tents were torn apart and belongings were tossed about like toys.

"Are you sure you want to see this?" asked Ward, looking into Carman's saddened eyes.

"I think we must, don't you?" she replied.

Ward took her by the hand and they walked into the encampment. Vultures with reddened eyes and powerful beaks defied them by waiting until the last minute before giving up the space they had taken over. The smell of burned flesh filled the air, while small areas of burning coals still smoldered.

"Is this where the massacre took place?" asked Carman, who had turned white around her eyes.

"If it's not the one Chief Broken Arrow told us about, then the Cavalry has struck again."

Vultures swooped down, coming dangerously close to Ward and Carman. The pounding of their wings were just overhead. Air from their mighty wings fanned the gray ash into a choking cloud.

"Will the vultures attack us?" inquired Carman, reaching for Ward's hand.

"I have never heard of it, but these creatures are angry with us."

Bodies mutilated by both the attackers and the vultures lay everywhere. While Ward looked over the burned area, Carman walked to a tent that was nearly intact and threw back the flap. "Oh, my Lord. Ward come over here quick."

Ward rushed to her side. Carman opened the flap once more and there standing inside was a small child. She looked numb and her eyes were filled with fear. Carman held her hands out to the child and walked slowly toward her. The child did not move, instead she stared beyond Carman.

"She's in shock," said Ward. "Now we don't want to frighten her anymore than she already is."

"She must be the only living thing left here."

"I would say you're right."

Carman dropped onto a buffalo robe laying on the ground. On her hands and knees she crawled closer to the child. "I don't believe she has blinked once since we got here," said Carman.

Ward sat down next to Carman and held his hands out to the child. "Come, we will not hurt you. No one is ever going to hurt you again, I promise you that."

"That's a lot to say."

"Yes, and I mean it," declared Ward, staring at the helpless child.

"Wait a minute," whispered Carman. "I have a small cloth with sugar in it with me; maybe she would like the taste of that."

"You could try. Anything we can do to break this spell I think we should do. However, I don't believe she'll ever be the same child she was before this happened. Can you imagine what she saw?"

"Oh, my," exclaimed Carman.

After removing a small piece of cloth from her pocket,

Carman laid it on the robe and unfolded it. The Indian Child had still not blinked her eyes. Wetting her finger, Carman placed it in the sugar then crawled to where the child was standing. Slowly she reached out and touched the sugar to the child's lips. "Her lips are like paper, Ward."

"Hard telling how long it has been since she's had water."

Carman wet a second finger and rubbed the moisture on the child's lips, following with a few grains of sugar. "I believe she blinked her eyes, Ward."

Ward returned from where he was standing at the tent opening. "You think she might have?"

"Yes."

After Carman's third attempt to put sugar on the child's lips, the little girl licked her lips and then again. Quietly Carman offered the child more sugar and said, "I can't see you, Ward, but she's licking the sugar."

"I'm behind you and I can see that, maybe she'll come around. However, we must be prepared to grab her. I would assume she'll try to run from us."

"But why? We are here you help her."

Ward gently placed his hand on Carman's shoulder. "We are her mortal enemy, and nothing is going to change that now."

Carman's patience was rewarded when the girl looked into Carman's blue eyes. Carman crawled closer. Reaching out she placed her hand on the child's cheek. "Is there some water out there, Ward?" she asked in a whisper.

"I'll see."

Ward was gone only a few minutes and returned with a small clay cup of water. Handing the cup to Carman, he stepped back and watched her touch the cup to the child's lips. The child opened her mouth slowly then gulped the water down.

"We had better watch her. She could run at any moment. I'll stand at the opening."

It wasn't long before Carman had the child sitting next to her and was holding the child in her arms.

"How old would you say she was?" asked Ward.

"It's really hard to tell. Her expressions are not that of a child as we know it."

"I can understand that after what she's just gone through."

"We can't leave her here, Ward."

"I have no intention of leaving her here. However, I must tell you when we get back to the wagons and Hawk sees what we have with us he'll look and sound like a wild man."

"I have no doubt about that, but I'm sure Emily will see to it that he calms down really quick."

"She does influence him whenever she wants to," chuckled Ward.

"We should be ready to leave before long," said Carman. "She seems to be comfortable with me."

"I'll put the fires out that are still burning."

"What about the bodies out there?" inquired Carman.

"If there are any of this tribe left, they will be back after their dead, and I don't want to be the one that touched them. The Indians take care of their own."

"I guess I understand, if I will ever understand their way of life."

"Believe me, it's easier for us to understand their way of life than it is for them to understand ours."

When Ward returned after putting the fires out, Carman got to her feet and took the little girl by the hand. "Will you come with me?"

The girl looked up into Carman's smiling face, then gripped Carman's hand.

Slowly they walked out of the tent and toward the horses. Vultures had swooped in once more and were on the ground, ripping and tearing at the bodies. Their bloody bills and faces were a sight of horror. Overhead circled many more ready to follow those on the ground.

Upon arriving where their horses were tied, the little girl tugged at Carman's hand while looking intently at something across the way. "What is it, child?" asked Carman.

"She wants to show you something," said Ward, walking behind them.

"But what?"

"I don't know, but if she feels a need to show you something then best you go with her."

"Will you come with us?" asked Carman.

Ward shook his head and followed the little girl through the burned out tents. Nearing what had been a large tent, the girl pointed to a body laying face down on the ground. With his foot, Ward rolled the body over. It was that of a woman. Bitterly the girl pointed.

"I suppose this is the body of her mother," said Ward, glancing at the child.

Carman dropped to her knees and caressed the child in her arms. "You poor thing. Is that your mother?" The girl was as stiff as a board. Hate consumed her face.

Ward reached out and touched Carman on the head. "We really must be leaving. Take your time, but remember we must not let her become angry with us." Ward walked back to where the horses were. Carman worked wonders with the child and after nearly a half hour, she had the child sitting with her on her horse ready to leave."

"It looks like you're ready," said Ward.

"As I ever will be."

Leading the way, Ward turned his horse and headed back toward the wagon train.

Carman took one last look. Vultures were still pecking and fighting among themselves over the half stripped carcasses.

"Don't torture yourself, Carman," said Ward.

"I will never forget this scene; I just can not believe my eyes."

"Come, Carman. We must hurry; darkness is about to fall upon us."

The three of them rode up and over the crest of the hill. There in the distance burned two large fires. It was the wagon train bedding down for the night.

"How are we coming?" asked Ward.

"Just fine, she seems to be relaxing some."

"I don't know how, but they are strong people," commented Ward.

A cheer went up when those of the train saw Ward and Carman entering the perimeter of light from the campfires. They were met by Hawk as they entered the compound. "Where in the hell have you been?"

"Please," said Ward, "not now, we have someone with us."

"Where they at?" shouted Hawk.

"Will you shut your damn mouth for once, Hawk," scolded Emily, appearing out of the shadows.

Carman stopped her horse. "Emily, will you come over here for a minute?"

Emily walked over to where Carman was still sitting on her horse. Carman slowly removed the blanket from the little girl and dropped it to the ground.

"Oh, my," said Emily. "What do we have here?"

"We found her in a burned out Indian camp some miles away."

Hawk puffed up and Emily slammed her foot on the ground. "Hawk, if you say one word, I'll walk back to Hannibal as sure as I'm standing here. There must be a reason for all of this and you're going to listen to what they have to say."

Emily held the little girl in her arms, waiting for Carman to dismount.

Hawk, minding his manners, took Ward by the shoulder and walked over to one of the fires. "What's this all about?"

"We found a burned out Indian camp and this child was the only living thing left there."

"You shouldn't have done this, Ward."

"What the hell were we suppose to do, leave her there to die?"

"If those Indians come back and have any idea the white man took one of their children, they will hunt us down if they have to follow us to California."

"Aren't you exaggerating a bit?" asked Ward.

"You'll think I'm exaggerating if they come after us."

Ward looked around. Carman, Emily and several other women were walking to Carman's wagon. Rather, Hawk agreed with what the women had done. He would have no chance coming down on Carman or Ward. Ward smiled at Hawk, "You know something?"

Hawk scowled. "What?"

"I think I would rather fight off the Indians than I would the women on this train."

"This is serious."

"I know it is, Hawk, but what is done is done and I would do it again—could you have left that child back there?"

"All right, men!" shouted Hawk, completely ignoring Ward. "Take your places for the night. We will change guards every two hours instead of three. I can't tell you how important it is to stay awake and keep alert. Do you hear me?"

In the meantime, Carman with Emily, was in Carman's wagon tending to the child when the front flap opened. Through the opening came a woman's voice. "Here is a small bowl of soup for the child and a larger one for you, Carman."

"I don't know that I can eat," said Carman, "but thank you anyway."

"Do try to eat," said the woman, closing the flap and returning to her wagon.

"She's right you know, Carman," said Emily. "And I suppose the child might eat better if you were to eat with her."

"You have a point there, Emily. I'll try."

It was difficult to get the child to eat the first bite. However, after that, she ate as if she were nearly starved. Carman shared her soup with the child until she turned her head away.

"There," said Carman. "Now if the little one will only sleep."

"She has to be exhausted," said Emily, "and with the warm food in her belly she should sleep."

"She seems to be comfortable with me," said Carman, wiping the hair out of the child's face.

Emily smiled, "Yes, and isn't she a pretty little thing."

"Oh, yes, I have never seen eyes so brown."

Carman laid the child on two soft blankets then curled up beside her. Emily waited until both Carman and the child were asleep then left for her wagon.

✦✦✦✦✦✦✦✦ CHAPTER NINE ✦✦✦✦✦✦✦✦

DAYBREAK OF THE FOLLOWING DAY opened up the eastern horizon. The sun rays below the earth's rim shown brightly against the dark gray mountains far to the west. Snow covered peaks glistened in the brightness of the sun and reflected on the small encampment readying itself for another day of travel over unforgiving lands.

Ward had gotten up early, wiped down his horse and saddled him for the ride. It was one of the few times his horse had been without his saddle since they left Hannibal and it had given him a chance to be free of men's' trappings.

After Ward had finished with his horse he hurried over to Carman's wagon and whispered from outside. "Are you awake?"

Carman appeared at the rear of the wagon looking out between the flaps. "Yes. It's all right; she's awake."

"Did you get any sleep?" inquired Ward.

"Some."

"How about the child?"

"She slept like a kitten. Woke up a couple of times then went right back to sleep."

"No doubt she has gone without sleep for days. " said Ward. Pity loomed over Ward's face.

"I know."

Ward looked into Carman's swollen eyes. "You're a wonderful person, Carman."

"What makes you say that?"

"I felt it had to be said."

"I liked hearing it."

Ward hesitated for a moment, then said, "Do you think the little girl would like some fresh milk?"

"Where would we get that?"

"One of Mrs. Worton's cows is still giving milk. I could ask her."

Carman smiled, "Why don't you do that." Ward started to walk away when Carman continued, "Ward, you are a fine man."

"Thank you, Carman."

Approaching Mrs. Worton, Ward said, "Could I milk a small amount of milk from your cow? The child is awake and we thought it might taste good to her."

"Well, of course, do you know which one it is?"

"I'm afraid I don't."

"See the one with her left horn bent down?"

"Yes."

"That's her, but maybe I had better milk her for you. She has been known to kick if she doesn't know you."

"I would appreciate it if you would."

Mrs. Worton jumped to the ground and with a pail in hand she walked over to where the cow was standing. "This must be done everyday anyway in order to keep her giving milk."

After Mrs. Worton had finished, she poured some milk in a tin and handed it to Ward. "If this is not enough, come back before we head out. There will be plenty left for the child after we are finished."

"Thank you, Mrs. Worton. I may be calling on you again."

"Anytime."

Ward hurried back with the warm milk and handed it to Carman through the rear flap. "If we need more, Mrs. Worton said we are welcome."

"She's a nice person, Ward. Too bad she had to lose her husband." With that, Carman disappeared into the wagon and Ward joined Hawk outside the circle.

"Where we heading today?" asked Ward.

"You see that humpback mountain over there to the south?"

"I see it."

"We will head due west and after about a half a day we'll veer southwest."

"How far would you say we are from the peak?" asked Ward.

Hawk smiled slightly. "About four days."

Ward snapped his head around. "Four days?"

"That's right. Of course we'll be into the foothills before that, but that mountain itself is about four days away from here."

"But it looks so close."

"Ward," said Hawk, "that's one hell of a large mountain out there."

"Well, I guess it must be."

Hawk removed his hat and slapped it against his leg. Dust flew and he returned it to his head. "How's that savage you brought back with you?"

"If you mean the little girl, she's doing all right according to Carman. I haven't seen the child yet this morning."

"All right, the child. I'm just glad I said that to you instead of saying it while Emily was around."

Ward chuckled to himself. "That Emily is like a cocklebur, when she gets onto you, you can't get her off."

"That's no damn lie, but Ward she is one fine woman. When she gets on me I usually have it coming. Now, I would call you a damn liar if you ever told anyone I said that."

"Don't worry about it, Hawk; we all have to unload once in awhile."

Hawk turned and looked to the west. "Let's break camp. We have miles to roll under these wagons today."

Hawk then rode down the line of wagons asking the same question, "How do you feel and is your equipment in shape?"

The settlers by then were a tough bunch and didn't lend themselves to much conversation, they were eager to get to California.

Ward, on the other hand, trotted his horse down to Carman's wagon and called out to her. "Are you all set to move out?"

"I believe so," she replied, poking her head out through the flaps.

"How's the child?" inquired Ward.

"The activity outside seemed to have her a bit upset, but she'll be all right."

"Did she drink her milk?"

"Oh, my yes, that tasted good to her."

Ward smiled. "It's time for me to go out on the point, but I'll see you this evening or before, if I have reason to come back in."

"Do be careful, Ward." Carman's forehead furrowed, "I don't want anything to happen to you."

"You know, Carman, that's the first time since I held my mother's apron strings that anyone has been concerned about my well being."

"That's hard to believe; someone must have cared."

"I left home at fourteen and that was the last I saw of my family."

"You been on your own since then?"

"Yes, Carman. A boy grows up pretty darn fast when he's alone in this world."

Carman smiled, "I do care about your well being as you put it and I'll be looking forward to seeing you when you come in for the night."

Ward tapped the beak of his hat and rode out through an opening between the wagon and headed west. Carman watched until the last puff of dust from Ward's horse laid itself down on the ground.

Just before going back into the wagon, Emily stepped up. "I couldn't help but hear you tell Ward that the child got through the night all right."

"Oh, yes, she did fine and did you hear the rest of our conversation?"

"Of course I did and it just warms my heart, Carman."

"Mine too, he seems like such a nice man."

"I think he is and if I were you I would keep a spot in my heart for him. But promise me one thing."

"What's that?"

"If he doesn't return your feelings in the right way, don't chase him to the ends of the earth just to be with him."

"I do believe I understand."

"You should; you have seen what has happened to me."

"You love Hawk, don't you, Emily?"

Emily dropped her head.

"There's nothing wrong with loving a man is there?" asked Carman.

"No, but he makes me live a life of sin and I wasn't brought up that way."

"I can't argue with that," remarked Carman, flashing a sympathetic smile at Emily.

Carman had spent the day caring for the little girl and was nearly numb to everything around her. The little girl had finally stopped her quivering and Carman felt as if a load had been taken off of her.

With the child in her arms, Carman left her wagon. After standing the child on the ground, Carman walked with her. A harsh scowl lined the little girl's face. Her hand was tense as she walked at Carman's side.

At the sound of horses hooves Carman looked up. Riding toward them was Ward. Her face beamed and Ward nodded to her. Dropping to the ground, Ward squatted down and looked into the little girl's eyes. "How has she been doing?"

Carman, still holding the little girl's hand, replied, "She has eaten well and slept most of the time."

"That's good. She needed both."

"Oh yes, and even though she is asleep she hangs on to my hand. Emily did stay with her for a while this afternoon, so that I could get out, stretch my legs and breathe in some fresh air. I'll be glad when we get to the river, she sure needs a bath."

"Don't you think we all feel this way?" commented Ward.

"Yes, but this is different."

"I think I know what you're talking about."

"Would you walk with us for just a minute. I like talking with you, Ward."

Ward then strolled with Carman up to where the men had built a fire. There Hawk was waiting for him.

"Will we see you later?" asked Carman.

"If you don't mind, I thought I would come down and we could have supper together."

Carman's smile showed weariness, yet there was happiness in her eyes. "I would like that." Carman looking down at the child, turned and started back to her wagon.

"What does it look like up there, Ward?" asked Hawk, stomping out a coal that had popped out of the fire.

"Much of the same for the next half a day and then the terrain gets rough, and I mean rough, Hawk."

"I think I know the stretch you're talking about. Isn't

there a river that crosses our trail up there?"

"That's it and I'll be surprised if all the wagons hold together during this leg of the trip."

"It's a test all right, but the ones you think will fall apart don't and the ones you think would hold together don't."

Moments later Leaky joined Hawk and Ward. "You mind if I say something, Hawk?"

"No, Leaky. Go ahead."

"I think we're being followed."

"Followed?" said Hawk.

"I sure do. Unless my eyesight has gone bad, there's been Indians staying just far enough back to look like shadows darting around behind us."

"How long has this been going on?" asked Hawk, coming straight up in his saddle.

"I noticed them about high noon."

"Why didn't you say something about it earlier?" shouted Hawk.

"Every time I have something to say to you, you don't pay any attention to me, so I said to myself, to hell with it."

"Why do you think I have you back there flanking us?"

Leaky stuck his nose in Hawk's face. "Why the hell don't you listen to someone beside yourself?"

Hawk, ready to cuss Leaky out, was stopped right in his tracks by Emily who had came up alongside Leaky. "He's right, Hawk, you're so darn busy being the boss around here you don't listen to anyone that has something to say."

"Now listen here, Emily."

"No, Hawk, you listen to me. It just can't be Leaky. I'm sure there are others that would rather face a sidewinder crawling along the ground than they would saying something to you."

"This is serious, Emily."

"I know that, Hawk, but if you hadn't put the fear of God in these people they could talk to you, so if we are in trouble it's your own darn fault."

"But Emily—"

"Don't 'Emily' me. I swear if I get back to Hannibal alive, I'm going to get my own wagon train and head West."

"I think you could do it, Emily," joined in Leaky.

"I am the wagon master and you'll do as I say."

"I intend to do that, only because I respect your position and that's all." Emily, red-faced, left in a huff and returned to her wagon.

"What do you do with a woman like that?" said Hawk.

"I know what I'd do," remarked Leaky.

"And what's that?" roared back Hawk.

"I'd listen to her once in awhile. She seems to make some good sense."

Hawk, raising his voice, pointed to Leaky's wagon, "Now you get back to your wagon, grab your rifle and take up a position in that rock formation just outside the perimeter of light."

"Who's going with me?" asked Leaky, looking back at Hawk a bit wild-eyed.

"No one is going with you. If there are Indians out there, it's because you let them come up on us and never said a word."

"It's not my fault they were following us."

"To hell it's not, if we could have confronted them in the daytime, chances are they wouldn't be with us tonight, if in fact they are. Now get going."

"I don't want to go out there alone. One of those savages could sneak up on me and have my throat cut before I knew it."

Hawk angrily responded, "That's right. But remember you put this whole wagon train in danger, now get out there and fire one shot if you see any Indians coming toward the wagons."

"It's all right, Leaky; I'll go with you. I can't blame you for being frightened." It was Emily, carrying a rifle nearly her size.

Hawk hearing Emily's voice whirled around and shouted, "You can't do that, Emily, you could get yourself killed."

"I can't see any difference if it would be me or Leaky that got killed out there."

"Well—well—"

"Stop your stuttering, Hawk, and answer my question."

"You're different, Emily."

"Can't see it that way. You're not really putting Leaky out there to protect us. You're doing it out of spite."

Hawk grabbed the hat off his head and slammed it on

the ground. "Now you look here, Emily, and anyone else that wants to listen. I'm running this train and by damn starting now; I am the wagon master in charge. I will not take anymore mouth from anyone, is that clear?'

"Do we go out there or don't we?" asked Emily.

"I said Leaky was going to be the rear guard and that is what he is going to be. If you want to go with him, then go." With that said, Hawk turned and stomped over to where Ward was standing.

"You do have to keep control, Hawk," said Ward.

"You're damn right I do. I don't know what has gotten into Emily lately. She just seems to be on the opposite side of the fence from me on everything that comes up."

"It would seem that way."

"Now you look here, Ward. You're not coming out of this clean, you know."

Ward swallowed. "I don't think I understand."

"That Indian Child you and Carman brought back is no doubt at the root of this."

"I still don't think I understand, Hawk."

"I would guess these Indians may be a band of hunting braves that were away from camp when the raid took place."

"So!"

"So just like anyone else, after taking a head count of the dead, they find themselves missing a child. Now does that make sense?"

"I guess you have shucked it right down to the cob, Hawk."

"I thought you would understand. But what has been done has been done. I couldn't have expected you to know. You really did the only humane thing that could have been done at the time."

"Thank you, Hawk."

Hawk ignoring Ward's remark ordered the men to build a second fire as big as they could make it, but to leave enough wood to keep it going all night."

"Will they attack tonight?" inquired Ward, watching the men pile wood on the fire.

"Not an all out attack, but I wouldn't put it past them to try and infiltrate our circle of wagons. I want you to go down the line and tell everyone to stay awake, except for the Indian Child. I want her to sleep if at all possible."

"I can see what you're getting at, but that doesn't make much sense to me."

"Didn't I just get through saying I am the last word on this wagon train?"

"Yes, you did, but I'm not one to be led around blindly."

"All right, get it off your chest."

"Why don't we just give the child back to them," asked Ward bluntly.

"We're not that sure this is the reason the band is here, now are we?"

"Well, no."

"If we gave the child up to an enemy of her tribe they could put her to death."

"Isn't that what you want?"

Hawk roared with anger, "No, that's not what I want."

"You as much as said that when we came into camp with her," snapped Ward, through gritting teeth.

"It may have sounded like that, but I never said I wanted the child dead. Did I?"

"No, Hawk, you didn't say it— Now I think I'll go see how everyone is getting along."

"Oh, by the way, Ward."

"What?"

"There are two families with yapping dogs. Tell them not to let the dogs curl up and go to sleep; they just may be our salvation."

Ward nodded his head and rode slowly around the circle of wagons, contacting each family, telling them what was in the wind. Both families with their dogs burst with pride, knowing they might just have something to do with the safety of the settlers that night.

During his ride, Ward watched Leaky and Emily until they disappeared into the night.

Before returning to where Hawk was waiting, Ward stopped at Carman's wagon. "Carman," he whispered.

"Yes, what is it?" she asked, poking her head through the opening in the canvas.

"Is the child asleep?"

"Yes, " she replied. "Why?"

"Whatever you do, don't wake her up. If there are Indians looking for her, Hawk doesn't want them to hear her."

"If there isn't a lot of noise, I think she'll sleep through the night. She is still awfully tired."

Meanwhile, Leaky and Emily slipped away into the darkness. The moon was a sliver of light, but did cast a dim light, allowing Leaky and Emily to find a ledge with a wall of granite to their backs. Tucking themselves between jagged rocks they prepared for a long and perhaps a dangerous night.

Shortly the moon dimmed and was gone. A large cloud bank moved across the skies and snuffed it out. From where they were sitting they could see the two fires burning brightly among the wagons. If anyone were to make a dash for the encampment, Leaky and Emily would be able to see them in the perimeter of light surrounding the wagons.

"How you doing, Emily?" whispered Leaky, grunting as he tried making himself comfortable.

"I'm fine, but it's going to be a long night."

"What's our chances of being attacked tonight?" asked Leaky.

"There will be no raid, but I wouldn't rule out the fact that some of the Indian braves may try to sneak into the compound."

"They're after that Indian Child, aren't they?" asked Leaky.

"I would expect, but there's no way to know what they are up to," replied Emily, laying her rifle in her lap.

CHAPTER TEN

AFTER A NIGHT OF FEAR, the encampment was brought to life by the light of day pushing aside the darkness. Through the eerie morning gray, appeared Leaky and Emily on their way back to the campsite. Ward was the first to meet them. Placing one arm around Emily, he walked with her over to where coals from the once roaring fire still glowed.

"This heat should feel good to you, Emily."

"Oh, yes," she replied, dropping to her knees and extending her hands toward the fire.

Ward touched her face with the back of his hand. "My, you are cold."

"Yes, that night air plus sitting with my back to that granite wall, I did get cold."

"Don't nobody want to know if I'm cold or not?" chirped Leaky, backing up to the fire.

"You're too mean to be cold," smiled Ward.

Hawk's large frame appeared from out of nowhere. "How'd it go, Leaky?"

"I think they were pretty darn close to us at one time. A few rocks rattled down from above, but I don't think they knew we were out there."

"I see you came through it all right, Emily."

"Yes, Hawk, I'll be all right as soon as I get myself warmed up."

"I'm going down and see about the child," said Ward, turning away from the fire.

Hawk with a soft and understanding voice said, "Let me know how things are going with the child and Carman."

Ward had taken a couple of steps when Hawk spoke up once more. "Oh, yes, Ward, don't be getting all moon-eyed when you see Carman."

Ward whirled around and came storming back at Hawk, "What did you say?"

"I guess I said something to make you mad," replied Hawk, a bit quieter than before.

"Yes, you did. The way I feel toward Carman is something special and I don't want her name ever mentioned in a tone other than respect....Do you hear me, Hawk?"

"Yes, Ward, I hear you and so does everyone on the wagon train."

"Well then, I guess that goes for all of them."

"You have made your point, Ward, now go on."

"Darn right he made his point," agreed Emily, harshly. "Maybe if some of you damn fool men would treat a woman the way Ward treats Carman, there wouldn't be so much clawing and fighting between the sexes."

"All right, all right, Emily. I don't want to hear about that all day," snarled Hawk.

Hawk glanced to the east then walked out between a couple of wagons. There he checked on those men who had been on guard duty last. The men were tired and were walking back and forth to keep themselves awake. "How'd it go, Mosley?" asked Hawk.

"All I can say is they never got this far."

"What do you mean by that?" inquired Hawk, looking into Mosley's weary eyes.

"They were all over out there, just beyond the perimeter of light."

"Are you sure?" asked Hawk.

"I could see their faces sometimes and what I thought was the reflection of knife blades in the crimson light from the fire."

"Why didn't you let someone know?"

"Did we have to fight 'em?" asked Mosley, looking out over the vast area to the north.

Hawk snapped at Mosley with an unsettled voice, "Well, no, but we could have."

After leaving Mosley, Hawk continued on, but when rounding one of the wagons to the east, something caught his eye. It was a body lying on the ground. Hawk hurried over to where the body lay and dropped to his knees.

Touching the body, he realized the settler was alive and rolled him over on his back.

It was Steward Clark. A blank stare gripped the victim's face. Hawk whipped out his knife and cut a piece of wet rawhide that had been tied tightly around Clark's neck. Clark coughed and tried to sit up, but he was tied at the ankles and his hands were tied behind his back. "What the hell happened here?" asked Hawk.

Clark, nearly out of breath and unable to talk, pointed to his mouth. His breath was short and quick.

"Water?" asked Hawk.

Struggling, Clark nodded his head. Hawk jumped to his feet and ran to one of the wagons where he grabbed a dipper of water and hurried back to where Clark was gasping.

"Here," said Hawk, "just take a little at a time. You need to wet yourself all the way down."

Clark, with shaking hands, grasp the tin cup and brought it to his lips. "Rinse your mouth out first," said Hawk, steadying Clark's head.

One by one, including Ward, settlers gathered around Hawk to see if there was anything they could do to help.

"What's up?" asked Ward, kneeling down by Hawk.

"Those redskins were here last night and this is their work."

"Is he hurt?"

"I don't think so. All they wanted to do is let us know they could come into our camp anytime they wanted to."

Clark, sitting up joined in, "I never saw them until they were on top of me. I have no idea where they came from."

"They'll do that," said Hawk. "And all I can say is that you're lucky they didn't cut your throat and leave you here to bleed to death."

Clark shuddered while still sitting on the ground leaning on one hand. Mrs. Clark then burst through the crowd and ran to her husband's side. "What has happened here?"

"I guess I served as a warning from the Indians."

Mrs. Clark joined her husband on the ground. "Did they hurt you?"

"If Hawk hadn't gotten to me when he did I don't think I would have made it."

Mrs. Clark threw her arms around his neck and wept,

"Thank God, he saved you."

"It's all right now, so maybe you had better get back with the children and remember, don't ever let them out of your sight," insisted Mr. Clark.

"I won't; I promise," sobbed Mrs. Clark, holding her skirt high, preparing to run to the children.

Hawk and Ward helped Clark to his feet and walked with him to his wagon where they sat him down on the wagon tongue. "Will you be all right?" asked Hawk, bending down and looking deep into Clark's eyes. They had cleared some and were not filled with the terror as they were when Hawk first came upon him.

Leaving the Clarks, Hawk and Ward made their rounds and found everyone was on edge and rightfully so. Hawk, trying to keep the panic down, spoke gently to the rest of the settlers telling them, "The wagon train will be leaving when the sun's first rays appear on the very tip of that mountain ahead. It's called the Devil's Peak."

After completing his rounds and returning to the campfire, Ward said, "You handled the situation very well, Hawk."

"Thank you, Ward. It's good to hear someone say I was something other than a yelling, cussing wagon master."

"You know, Hawk, everyone has a certain talent that seems to come out during times like this and you found yours."

"Guess I did, Ward. You know, it felt good."

"We could use more of that from you, Hawk."

"Damn it, Ward. I can't do that."

"Well—"

Interrupting, Hawk explained, "This is a fine bunch of people we have with us on this trip. However, the next trip could be a different story."

"I guess I can understand that," said Ward. "But what are you going to do when Emily heads up her own wagon train leaving out of Hannibal and perhaps beats you to California someday?"

"You may laugh, but out of all the wagon masters working out of Hannibal, damn if she isn't the one I would figure could beat me someday."

"It doesn't have to be that way, Hawk."

Hawk looked down and at his side stood Emily. "Don't keep sneaking up on me like that. Sometimes I think you have Indian blood in your veins."

"Would that make any difference in the way you feel toward me?"

"Emily, you have got to stop talking like that."

"I'll keep talking like this until you admit I'm something more than one of those mules standing over there."

Ward was smiling from ear to ear watching Emily, a mite of a woman, dress Hawk down and put him in his place.

"Emily, we don't have time for this. We have a wagon train to get to the West Coast and you know that."

"All right, but it's only for these dear souls that are so eager to get moving." Emily spun on her heel and headed for her wagon.

Hawk shook his head, "Get 'em ready to move out."

Ward trotted his horse the length of the train inquiring if everyone was ready to continue on. On his way back, he looked in on Carman and the Indian Child. "How's she doing and how are you doing?"

Carman smiled. "I never dreamed of becoming a mother so quick and in such a strange place."

"You'll make a good one, Carman."

"Now to answer both your questions, we're both doing just fine."

"Remember, she's untamed and she could make a break for the wild in the blink of an eye."

"Do you think she would do that?"

"It's very possible."

"But she seems to be so content with me."

"I realize that and she is; however, if the wild calls she will go."

"Oh my," exclaimed Carman, caressing the little girl in her arms.

Ward laid the reins to his horse's neck and rode off, remembering the wave Carman had just given him.

"Ward," shouted Hawk, as Ward on his anxious steed rode by.

"Yes, Hawk, what is it?" said Ward, returning to where Hawk was standing.

"When you come to the river we spoke of, ride on back here and let me know."

Ward acknowledged by raising his hand, then rode out leaving a cloud of dust lingering.

"Move 'em!" shouted Hawk, motioning with his hand held high in the air.

The sound of wagons creaking, cattle mooing and children laughing, painted a picture of courage the settlers were made of.

Hawk waited until Leaky brought up the rear and rode alongside him. "Leaky, if you see anything that doesn't look right to you, make it known. I think we were just lucky to get out of last night with only Mr. Clark being roughed up a bit."

"You ain't gonna get mad if I tell you something and it turns out to be nothing, are you?"

"Leaky, nothing is going to hurt us now, but something could along the way. So if you see something we'll get together and decide what to do. Is that understood?"

"You bet it is, Hawk. Sure glad we had this talk."

"Maybe I should have said something before." Hawk didn't wait for a reply, instead, he strapped his horse on the rump and galloped off.

At the head of the column Hawk surveyed the surroundings. The sun was bearing down on them and was going to cook up a hot day. The warmest day they would encounter since they left Hannibal. A thin layer of clouds hung overhead and to the west a large black cloud loomed high over the mountains. The wind was constant and without gusting. Far to the northeast, the skies were nearly black with vultures.

Hawk's only thought was that of the burned out Indian camp. With each hour the trail became cluttered with broken wagons that had become part of the hazardous trail and marked the way with heartbreaks and disappointment. There were skeletons of cattle heads that were scattered along the way and belongings of previous settlers had been left behind for various reasons.

Horses, oxen and mules were becoming frustrated as they were asked to move wagons over jagged rocks and over inclines making the weight they were pulling nearly a dead lift.

Suddenly the wagon belonging to the Hineburg's lurched. The left front wheel had broken. The wagon flipped over on its side and slid halfway down a rugged slope. The weight of the wagon and contents jerked the six oxen off their feet and sent them tumbling into a ravine below. Men and women looked on in horror. Mrs. Worton with the Indian Child's hand in hers, cried out, "Oh, good Lord, Mrs. Hineburg was in that wagon."

When the train came to a halt, Hawk roared, "You two women and a couple of you men try to free Mrs. Hineburg. The rest of you cut those oxen loose and get them on their feet as quickly as possible. They're down, but we don't want them to stay down."

Two men, along with Emily and Carman tried desperately to save Mrs. Hineburg from being crushed, while others worked to free the oxen and get them to their feet.

Hawk with one giant leap landed at the foot of the slope and pushed his way by those trying to free Mrs. Hineburg. "Mrs. Hineburg, can you hear me?" shouted Hawk.

"Yes," was her weak reply.

"I know you're in pain and before we get you out of here it is going to be worse, do you understand?"

"Yes, I hear you."

"Remember why you're here. You and your family are out here to start a new life. If you can think of that, it will help keep your mind off what's going on about you."

"I'll try."

"All right, men, start unloading that wagon. We've got to get as much weight off Mrs. Hineburg as possible before we attempt to lift the wagon." Hawk looked up to the crest of the hill and yelled. "Leave the oxen there and get down here. We're going to need all the hands we can get on this wagon."

The men on top of the hill scrambled down the slope and rushed to where Hawk was standing. "Now," called out Hawk, "don't anyone get between the wagon and the downside of the slope. When we lift this brute it's apt to roll and end up in the gully."

Positioning themselves, the men waited for Hawk's command. "All right, men, heave!" After lifting with all their might, the wagon rocked, then came back down. Mrs. Hineburg cried out with pain.

"Men," shouted Hawk, "don't let that happen again or Mrs. Hineburg will not come out of this alive. Do you hear me?"

The men shook their heads and positioned themselves once more. Hawk with his shoulder to the wagon box, called out. "Hit it and don't you dare let it back down again." Faces reddened. Men's muscles strained beyond their ability.

"Come on, men!" shouted Hawk once more. "I can't move this thing all alone."

The rest of the men, angered by what Hawk said, called on every bit of strength they had in their bodies. The wagon started up. "All right, men, when I say let her go, jump back; it may come our way again."

Emily and Carman waited anxiously to go to Mrs. Hineburg's aid. In their minds and very souls they could feel every agonizing lift made by each man.

"Let her go, boys!" shouted Hawk, scrambling out of the way. Teetering at midpoint the wagon finally tipped and went tumbling and rumbling down the slope, crashing into a wall of granite. Some men dropped to their knees while others stood with stooped shoulders staring at the crumpled wagon below.

Hawk, with Mr. Hineburg at his side, rushed to Mrs. Hineburg. Emily looked into her eyes and then up at Hawk. With a slight nod she stepped back, allowing Mr. Hineburg to go to his wife. Hawk stood back. Emily slipped her sweaty hand into Hawk's and dropped her eyes. Carman went to Mr. Hineburg and placed her hand on his shoulder. "Take all the time you need. We'll be here when you need us."

Mr. Hineburg looked up into Carman's wet eyes. "We did all we could do, didn't we?"

"Oh, yes. It really was all over before we moved the wagon, but everyone tried."

"You're good people and so was she. Thought we were going to have a lifetime together, but I guess that wasn't meant to be."

"I can't tell you I know how you feel because I don't,"

said Carman, kneeling down by Mr. Hineburg and taking him by the hand.

"I don't know how I feel; all I can hope is that I am as strong as Mrs. Worton has been after her loss."

"She should be a great help to you."

"I think so."

Carman waited for a moment and then said, "We must go, Mr. Hineburg. Please take my hand."

"But why?"

"There is nothing more we can do here on earth, but to give her a burial. She is now in the hands of Almighty God."

"May I have just a minute longer?"

"Yes, Mr. Hineburg, but please don't stay and suffer; we'll be waiting for you on the trail," whispered Carman softly in his ear.

Mr. Hineburg reached up and placed his hand on Carman's, still resting on his shoulder.

It wasn't long before Mr. Hineburg slowly climbed the slope and joined the others. "What's next, Hawk?"

"Do you see someplace you might want her buried?" asked Hawk, with kindness in his voice.

"No, for it will only be her body. I'll take her away in my memory."

"Do you want some words said over her, Mr. Hineburg?"

"I don't think so; I said a few words down there."

"We don't want you to feel later that you should have had some kind of a funeral," said Hawk firmly.

"I know what you're saying, Hawk, and I can assure you I'll have no misgivings."

With Mr. Hineburg at Emily's side, she walked with him to her wagon. "Why don't we just sit down and talk. Maybe there is something you would like to say."

"I don't believe I have anything to say, but I'll sit down."

Joining him, Emily said, "I can assure you I'm a good listener."

"I wouldn't have any problem telling you anything. It's just that it's over and now I must go on."

"That's a good way to look at it."

Meanwhile, a detail of men buried the body, while others transferred what belongings could be loaded into other wagons.

Before leaving, other settlers offered Mr. Hineburg space in their wagons for times when shelter would be needed.

Over Mr. Hineburg and Emily was cast a long shadow. Emily looked around. It was Hawk. "We must be going, Mr. Hineburg. Do you think you're ready to leave?"

With tear filled eyes, Mr. Hineburg looked up at Hawk. "I'll never be ready to leave her, but I know there is nothing more I can do." Staring at the mound of dirt that was Mrs. Hineburg's grave, he sniffled, "I don't think I told her I loved her this morning."

Mrs. Worton, who had turned the Indian Child back to Carman, heard what Mr. Hineburg had said, then spoke to him kindly, "There will be many questions you'll ask of yourself. Any answer you come up with will always be unclear. All I can say is don't punish yourself; it will do you no good and you will lose your worth to everyone you come in contact with."

Mr. Hineburg took Mrs. Worton by the hand. "I know you speak with wisdom. I only hope I can be as strong as you have been."

"We must go, Mr. Hineburg," said Hawk.

"I'm ready," he replied, striking out with long strides toward the head of the column. "By the way Hawk, if there comes a time you need someone to step into a dangerous situation, please promise you will call on me?"

Hawk looking down from his mount replied, "That's darn nice of you. We'll see if and when the time comes." Hawk then spurred his horse on and shouted to the rest. "Move 'em out. The next stop is the Green Water River, dead ahead."

Mr. Hineburg looked back, then with whip in hand he drove his oxen, still carrying their yokes, behind the wagons rumbling on ahead.

A second wagon that day broke a tongue; however, it was repaired and the wagon train moved on.

The time was late afternoon when Ward thundered in from the point and rode up alongside Hawk. "The Green River is just beyond that ridge over there. Are we going to make camp there for the night?"

"Yes, Ward. Now you go back and ride the river bank in

both directions. I don't want to camp near some Indian encampment."

Ward started to leave when he looked up in time to see Carman waving to him. He removed his hat and waved back before heading out. Carman smiled to herself and looked down at the child holding her hand. The child was looking back at Carman with dreamy eyes. Carman tied the reins together and placed them around her back. Reaching down, she picked the Indian Child up in her arms and walked slowly alongside her two teams.

Suddenly the trail was without jagged rocks and ruts. The wagon train moved on making better time then they had for several days.

Hawk had pulled away from the column and was riding far south as if looking for something. Reaching the crest of a hill, Hawk's silhouette against the skyline was tall and erect. Slowly a cloud of dust rose up beyond the hill and drifted east and high into the sky. As the cloud of dust thinned, he rode back to the train and then out front.

Hawk lead the wagon train into a sharp turn. The Green River lay dead ahead. A green lush meadow sprawled out from the river bank. Tall grass blowing in the wind swayed, reminding the settlers of fields of golden grain back East during mid-summer. Hawk raised his hand in the air and motioned for the wagons to form their nighttime circle. By this time camping was a maneuver done without thought.

Hawk called everyone to the river bank. "As soon as Ward comes in and tells us everything is clear, we're going to use this time as playtime. The river is clear and clean. You may water your livestock, wash clothes and even take a bath if you wish."

Ward then appeared coming from the north at a leisurely pace. "Everything is clear in each direction, Hawk."

"All right, folks. Water your livestock downstream and wash your clothes right here at the water's edge. Now if you ladies want to take a bath, Emily will take you to an area where you can bathe without fear of being seen. You men can wait until the ladies are finished before going into the water."

The camp was a beehive of activity. Clothes were being washed while men drove their livestock downstream where they could drink and walk in the river. Horses shoved their noses far into the water and came up snorting and shaking their heads. The water felt good to both man and beast.

Once the chores were done Emily accompanied the women upstream to a quiet bend in the river. There they bathed and frolicked in the water like children. Returning to camp in clean clothes, the women fussed, combing each others hair. They were all eager to look pretty again. The children played in the river until they were called to eat.

After they had eaten, men with their ladies in their arms, listened to a mournful harmonica playing a song pleasing to the ear. When the harmonica player picked up the beat, most of the couples jumped to their feet and danced. From the fireside, Hawk with Emily at his side said, "They will be tired in the morning, but tonight they are without worry."

"Don't know why we can't dance?" said Emily, looking up at Hawk.

"Emily, I'm the wagon master and I cannot get close to any of them out there. Who knows what tomorrow will bring and who I might have to come down on. I don't want to make friends, Emily, can't you see that?"

"I must admit you're right, Hawk. It's your job to get these people to California."

"Thank you, Emily."

Near the river, sitting on a grassy knoll, Ward and Carman looked up at the stars. Carman spoke in whispers, "It seems like I have known you for such a long time."

Ward leaned toward her. "It does feel that way and I like it."

"Me too."

"Do you have plans for when we arrive in California?" asked Ward.

"I'm going out to start a new life, and you?"

Ward cleared his throat, "I guess I'd have to say the same."

"Were you in the war, Ward?"

"Yes, why do you ask?"

"I thought you might be. You have a certain discipline about you."

"I didn't know it showed."

"Oh, yes, but I like it."

"How do you know about the war and soldiers?"

Carman lay back and looked up into the star studded skies. "I was a nurse."

"You were? Where?" exclaimed Ward.

"In Tennessee and Kentucky."

Ward on one elbow, leaned over and looked into her eyes. "I was in the battle of Franklin."

Carman gasped. "You were? I was in a field hospital north of there. Were you injured?"

"No, I came out without a scratch."

"Oh, I'm so glad."

There came a pause in their conversation then Carman said, "What are we going to do about the child?"

"She has been on my mind all day. She would never be accepted if we took her into our world."

Carman too, came up on one elbow. "Then what do we do?"

"I'm thinking about trying to find some tribe that would take her with a guarantee they would not harm her."

"Could we trust them?"

"I said I would try and find some tribe to take her. You will have to go on with the wagon train."

"I'll not go without you. Furthermore, I have a wagon and supplies and you have nothing"

"This could be a dangerous trip. We could be done in by some tribe before we could tell our story."

"I can't help it; I don't want you out there alone. And one more thing, I think they would believe the two of us before they would believe you alone."

Ward paused and looked out over the water. A crimson light from the campfires danced on the rippling river. The water rushed by, licking at the sandy banks. Music from the harmonica echoed down a nearby canyon and softly faded away. "You ever wonder who hears the last sound of an echo before it dies? I always have."

"What made you say that?" asked Carman, patting Ward's hand.

"I guess because I didn't have an answer for you."

"You don't need an answer. I want to go with you."

"I just don't know," pondered Ward quietly.

Carman rolled over on her stomach, placed her chin in her hands and looked up. "Ward, we are two people with no past or future as far as each other are concerned. So if something should happen to us on such a mission, then whose loss would it be?"

"You have a point. No one knows if I'm dead or alive," remarked Ward, running his fingers through Carman's hair.

"That's just the way with me. I have no parents, so what is there?"

"I have no parents, either," countered Ward. "That's why I ran away and joined the Army....Now that's as far as I want to go with my past."

"I respect that, Ward, and I ask that you not inquire about my past."

Slowly the clouds opened up and above them was a clear cold moon shinning down on them. Brightly it shown and Carman's eyes twinkled.

Ward lay down by Carman, lifted her chin and kissed her.

"Just one kiss?" she asked, stretching toward Ward.

A passionate kiss ensued, carrying them into a night of sheer fantasy.

When the sound of the harmonica died down, Carman and Ward joined the others near one of the glowing fires.

As the others disbursed, Ward said to Hawk, "I'll not be going on with you in the morning."

Hawk looked up, his shadowed face was stern. "What was that?"

"I said I'll not be going on with you. Carman and I are going to head out in the morning. We want to find either the Indian Child's tribe or some other tribe that will take her and raise her."

Hawk looked at Carman. "You do?"

"That's right, Hawk."

"You could get yourselves killed out there."

Ward took Carman by the hand. "We know that and are willing to take that chance."

"For just one child?"

"That's right," agreed Carman, squeezing Ward's hand

tightly.

"There's nothing I can say to change your minds?" asked Hawk, stubbornly kicking sand into the fire.

"We have made up our minds, Hawk," said Ward.

"You're leaving me without a scout," countered Hawk.

Out of the darkness walked a shadowed figure. "I'll be your point man."

Hawk strained his eyes. "Emily, what the hell are you doing out here."

"I just came to tell you I would be your point man."

"You can't do that," was Hawk's loud response.

"Why not? There isn't one man here other than Ward that could be on the point. Now, that leaves one person and that's me "

"You can't go out on the point, Emily."

"Who you got?"

Hawk ripped his hat off and threw it to the ground and shouted. "I've got me. I'll ride that point and if you think you are so damn good at being a wagon master, you can take over that job."

"Does that mean I'm the wagon boss?"

"No, damn it— well yes, but only when I'm not here."

Ward's eyes sparkled, watching Hawk and Emily going at it. "Hawk, I'm sorry I have to do this to you. All I can say is that I hope you understand."

"Well, I don't and this is leaving me in an awful spot."

"Hang it up, Hawk. We have always been a team and we still can be. Furthermore, I think Ward and Carman are doing the right thing in spite of what you say or think," snapped Emily.

Hawk looked at Ward, "I'm going to bed, and come morning I don't want either one of you getting in our way, do you hear me?"

"I don't want you to feel this way, Hawk. We've been friends and I would like to have it continue that way."

"If it doesn't, it's not my fault," replied Hawk, stomping toward the center fire where his bedroll was laid out.

Emily watched Hawk walk dejected toward the fire, then looked up at Ward. "You know, Ward, this is one hell of a spot to leave Hawk in."

"I know that, Emily, but do we have a choice?"

Emily with mixed emotions spoke up, "No, Ward, you don't have a choice; you must do this. However, it hurts me to see Hawk put in this position."

"We don't like doing this, Emily," explained Carman.

Emily turned and started to walk away. "I know you don't."

CHAPTER ELEVEN

DAYBREAK WAS UPON THE CAMP and a strip of orange lined the eastern horizon. The moon still lingered in the skies when Ward helped Carman hitch her teams to her wagon. Ward had filled the water barrels with clean cold water and they were ready to pull out.

"Hold it up, Ward."

Ward, ready to swing himself onto the wagon seat, looked around. It was Hawk. "All I can say, Ward, is take it slow and make damn sure you have your back to the wall at all times. Even I wouldn't want to be undertaking this journey."

Ward took Hawk's strong hand. "I was wondering if I would see you before we left. I hope our paths will cross somewhere along the way."

Hawk stepped back and gave Ward a wave. Carman alongside Ward, held the Indian Child close to her side.

With Ward handling the reins, Carman's wagon rumbling away caused a stir in the camp. Voices hummed as the word spread of their leaving.

Meanwhile, Ward and Carman headed north over the rolling plains. Daylight had caught up with them and the sun warmed their chilled bones. The route Ward had planned had not been traveled to any degree by the white man; therefore, every step the horses took was new territory and filled with the unknown. Ward realized he was not a seasoned traveler and that pitfalls could lay ahead of them that he was not aware of.

Carman leaned forward with her forearms on her knees. "There is no way to tell how far we will have to travel is there?"

"No, Carman, there's not, but we must remain alert to all

things around us. If you could watch the crest of the nearby hills around us for any sign of Indians, I'll scan the area ahead of us."

"I'm a little nervous," said Carman, wiping the hair off her forehead, then reaching down and hugging the Indian Child.

"After what I went through in the war, Carman, it takes a lot to unnerve me."

"I expect it would. I wasn't on the front lines as you were."

"We're going to get through this all right, then we're heading for California," was Ward's encouraging remark.

Moving north, they were able to follow a valley winding between mountain peaks to the east and the west. In the meantime, Ward had mounted his horse and had taken the lead.

The child sat with Carman on a hard wooden seat, clinging to Carman's skirt. It was dusk when Ward rode back to Carman's wagon and said, "There's a clump of trees just over that hill. Could be water nearby, so why don't you stay here while I ride on ahead and see what I can find."

"Be careful, Ward, and don't be long. I feel so all alone out here even with you."

Ward rode on, disappearing over the crest of a nearby hill. Carman's heart beat in her throat and perspiration stood out at her temples. She placed her arms around the child and brought her close. "It will be all right, little one. Ward is a very smart man and he'll be back soon."

It became deadly quiet. The only sound was that of the tall grass rustling in a gusty breeze blowing in from the west. Carman felt her heart thumping in her chest. She had never felt so all alone. A large shadow startled her as it moved swiftly across the ground ahead of her. She looked up. A bird, a very large bird, soared high overhead. Watching the graceful bird in flight, she followed his shadow speeding across the grassy valley and then up the mountainside where it disappeared.

Carman looked down. The child had lay her head in Carman's lap and was sound asleep. The world was no longer her friend or enemy. Carman stretched the child's legs out on the seat and let her sleep. Still gazing at her,

Carman couldn't help but think. This child could be mine and regardless where she came from she needs love.

"Oh, yes," she thought, "I couldn't pass her off as my child for people would know in a minute she was of Indian blood."

Carman looked beyond the child's reddish brown skin and her straight black hair. She looked beyond her brown eyes, dark eyelashes and high cheek bones and saw a beautiful child who was not filled with hate. Carman smiled when she thought what a dirty little thing the child was when they found her and how sparkling clean she looked after her bath in the river the previous night.

Slipping out from under the child's head, Carman climbed to the ground. There she walked to each of her horses and rubbed them on their jawbones. The horses stood calm. While standing at the head of the horses, one of them snorted and raised his head. His ears stood high and alert. Carman turned quickly and over the hill rode Ward at an alarming speed.

"What is it?" shouted Carman, as Ward rode up.

"Nothing, why?"

"You rode up so fast."

"My horse has been walking all day, so I let him run for a ways."

Carman patted her chest. "My, I thought something was chasing you."

Ward dropped to the ground and took Carman in his arms. "I'm sorry; I shouldn't have frightened you that way."

"That's all right."

"Where's the child?" inquired Ward.

"She just woke up and is in the wagon. I don't know what she's doing in there. Maybe we should take a peek."

Ward with Carman at his side walked to the wagon and opened the canvas. There on the floor was the little girl curled up like a kitten. The light shown in on her soft brown cheeks. Stretching some, she sighed, then settled down once more and drifted back to sleep.

Carman's eyes reflected a hurt.

"What is it, Carman?"

"I love that child."

"Don't become too attached to her," said Ward, closing

the flap.

"I don't know what I'll do when we have to give her up."

"You're a strong person, Carman."

"I don't know if I'm strong enough for that."

"But, Carman, we will take her back to her people where she belongs."

"You don't know that, Ward. You said if we couldn't find her tribe we would try and find a tribe that would take her in."

"That's right, now let's move on. There's a small river just ahead with an area of scrub trees. It will be a ideal place to camp for the night."

"That sounds like a nice spot," smiled Carman, placing her foot on the hub of the front wagon wheel.

"Here, don't get on yet," said Ward.

Carman turned and found herself locked in Ward's arms, with his lips pressed tightly to hers. Her hat fell to the ground and she grew limp. "Oh, my," she exclaimed, as their lips parted.

"Yes, I know."

"Maybe we had better find that little place of yours and make camp."

With that, Ward slipped his hands around her waist and helped her onto the wagon.

Ward mounted his horse and looked back at Carman. "You want to look in on the child?"

Carman turned on the seat and looked in through the flaps. Coming out smiling, she whispered, "She's still all curled up, bless her heart."

Ward waited until Carman had the reins gathered in her hands then touched his horse gently in the sides.

Moving forward, the wagon creaked then rumbled over the grassy plain. Reaching the crest of the hill, Carman looked on with astonishment for below them lay the river Ward had spoke of, along with the clump of trees green with foliage. Reaching the river bank, Ward dropped to the ground and tied his horse to a small bush. Carman with a broad smile on her face brought her teams up and parked her wagon parallel to the river. "How's this?" she asked, smiling down at Ward.

"That's fine," Ward hesitated, then pointed to the wagon.

Carman turned around. Peering out through the canvas flaps was the Indian Child looking out with sleepy eyes.

"Come on dear," said Carman, holding her hands out to the child. The little one reached up and Carman took her in her arms.

"Here, let me take her while you get down," said Ward, walking over to the wagon.

The child turned away and laid her head on Carman's shoulder. "Maybe we should wait until she wakes up. What do you think?"

"That's a good idea, but don't you want to feel the earth under your feet? You have been on that wagon for a good part of the day."

"Perhaps you're right." After the child lifted her head, Carman wrapped the reins around the brake handle, then with the child still in her arms she swung herself off the seat, onto a wheel hub, then to the ground. "My, that does feel good, but I still feel like I'm moving."

Ward chuckled, "That will no doubt go on all night."

"I'm afraid you're right," smiled Carman, strolling toward the river. "My, this is peaceful here."

"Should be a good place to camp," agreed Ward, stretching his arms and legs.

Carman sat the child on the ground then walked with her to the water's edge. There she kicked off her boots and with the child, stepped into the water. The child looked up and for the first time smiled at Carman. "Did you see that?"

"Yes, I did. She actually smiled, didn't she?"

Encouraged by the smile, Carman laughed out loud and threw her head back looking straight up to the heavens. "I have a feeling about this child, Ward."

"Like what?"

"I think the good Lord sent her to me."

"Now, Carman."

"But I really do. How come she was the only one to live through that awful attack? To me it is beyond coincidence."

"I'll collect some firewood while you try to relax for awhile."

Carman tossed her hair. "I don't see that you've been relaxing all day."

Ward smiled back at Carman. "That's all together different."

"Perhaps."

Soon a small, but roaring fire burned before them, adding to the pleasantness of their campsite. Carman with the child at her side started preparing the evening meal.

Darkness had moved in on them before they had eaten. After they had finished Carman washed the tins in the river and returned them to the wagon. Upon her return, Ward took her by the hand and with the child they walked to the river and sat at the water's edge. The rippling water moved swiftly downstream. A coolness from the cold water sent a chill up Carman's back.

"Do you want to turn in for the night?" asked Ward.

"I think so. I'm very tired."

"You sleep in the wagon with the little one and I'll sleep next to the fire."

Carman reached out and touched Ward's hand. "I hate to be so close without being close."

"I feel the same way...."

Carman gripped Ward's hand. "There will be time for that."

"There will?"

"Yes, Ward, I promise."

Ward accompanied Carman and the child back to the wagon where he stayed until he was sure they were settled in for the night. Returning to the fire, he laid his bedroll out. Small logs crackled and dancing flames reflected off the trees growing nearby. The night by then was pitch black.

With the sound of rushing water in the background and the crackling of the fire burning, Ward drifted off to sleep.

Suddenly Ward awoke and came up on one elbow. The horses were uneasy. Stomping their hooves, they pulled against the saplings to which they were tied. Ward jumped to his feet and joined the horses. One by one he stroked their faces and spoke softly to them.

While standing with the horses, Ward saw the red eyes of wolves pacing back and forth at the outer perimeter of light from the fire. Checking the horses' reins he found them secure. Returning to the fire, he threw on all the wood he had. While peering into the darkness, he found they were surrounded on three sides. He saw no signs of the animals between him and the river to his back.

Ward knew nothing of wolves and how they reacted. The only thing he ever heard was the gruesome stories passed on to him while he was a young lad growing up. The wood he had placed on the fire burst into flames sending the perimeter of light far beyond where it had been earlier. Slinking wolves retreated, but only to the edge of the light. The wolves being farther away, gave Ward some breathing room and a chance to get to the wagon.

"Carman," he whispered. "Are you awake?"

The flap opened, "Yes, what is it?"

"We're nearly surrounded by a pack of wolves."

"Oh, my!"

"Get your rifle and ammunition, then come on out."

"All right."

Ward had turned away, but stopped. "How is the child?"

"She is sound asleep."

"I was hoping for that," said Ward.

It was but a moment before Carman jumped to the ground. With her rifle in hand and a bag of ammunition, she hurried to Ward. "What's next?"

"You stand with your back to the horses. They'll let you know if the wolves are coming up on you. I'll stand at the fire in clear view."

"I want to be near you. I think we can protect each other if we have to," pleaded Carman.

"Stay with the horses, Carman. We need them and they need you."

Taking his position near the fire, Ward's keen eyes peered into the darkness once more. The wolves, like vultures, dared to come ever closer defying the roaring fire and the light reaching into the dark of night.

Carman, with her rifle cradled on one arm, felt her heart pounding at her temples. Her mouth grew dry and she licked at her lips. The horses held their heads high and watched with ears pointing straight ahead. Nervously they stomped their feet and snorted.

Ward standing firm suddenly looked up. The clouds had moved off swiftly, leaving behind a full moon, crystal clear in all its splendor. Carman receiving a motion from Ward hurried to his side.

"What is it?"

"It looks like they are now in a pack. Can you see their shadowy figures just to your left?"

"Yes, they look like a black mass."

"That's it. I don't know if they are preparing for an attack, but if they do attack, run to the wagon. If we need to fight them off, you'll be safer there and so will the child."

"I can't leave you out here, Ward."

"You must; we have no choice."

Carman pleaded with Ward. "Please come to the wagon with me."

"I'll stay with the horses, now you hurry."

She ran to the wagon, sprang to the seat, then disappeared in through the canvas flap.

In the meantime, Ward had taken up a position between the fire and the horses. A lonesome call from a wolf in the distance echoed throughout the darkness. An answering call from a nearby wolf shattered the night, sending a chill like a steel shaft up Ward's spine. The calls and the answers continued for some time. Then as they had come, the wolves with their tails low slinked away into the night.

Ward waited until he was sure the animals were gone before returning to the wagon. "Carman, you may come out; they've left."

Carman appeared. "Are you sure?"

"Reasonably sure."

She joined Ward on the ground, then walked with him to where the horses were tied. "They seem to be rather calm now," she commented.

"Yes, and that gives me more reason to believe the beasts have gone for the night."

Ward looked up into the flawless skies. "Must be shortly after midnight, so why don't you go back to the wagon and get the sleep you need."

"I'm not going until I'm sure you're going to lie down and rest."

"One of us must stay awake, Carman."

"Then let it be me. It will be more important for you to

be alert tomorrow than me."

"Please, we don't have time to discuss this," insisted Ward.

Carman dropped her eyes, then returned to the wagon.

Ward, laying on the ground between the fire and the horses, dozed off. He was unaware how long he slept when the horses once more reared up and thrashed at the end of their reins. Ward leaped to his feet in time to see several balls of fire sizzling through the night. The first landed near the wagon before he realized they were flaming arrows. A second flaming arrow pierced the wagon canvas. Ward ran frantically and jumped on the wagon. Throwing back the flap he shouted, "The wagon is on fire! Hurry, Carman, give me the child."

With the child in his arms, he jumped to the ground, followed by Carman. She had no more hit the ground when she was back in the burning wagon, coming out with her rifle, handgun and shells.

Ward grabbed a wooden bucket and ran to the river, coming back with it filled to the brim. The blaze had opened a large hole in the side of the canvas. Ward drenched the flames and returned to the river. While he was gone, several more burning arrows landed on the wagon and in dry grass nearby. Realizing when he returned that it would be impossible to put the fire out, they retreated and watched the flames consume Carman's belongings. Angered, Ward fired several rounds into the night. A deafening roar split the silence, followed by a blue flame bursting out of his rifle barrel.

Carman, unaware that Ward was planning on firing, jumped and screamed at the top of her voice.

Ward rushed to her side. The Indian Child was crying. "What is it?" he shouted.

"I didn't know you were going to fire."

"I didn't have time to say anything."

"I know that, but now what do we do that we have lost everything?"

Dejected, Ward stood with his rifle hanging loose in his hand. "I don't know...." He paused then whispered, "Listen."

Out of the night came a shriek, then another. It was Indians celebrating the burning of a settler's wagon.

Moments later there were the sounds of thundering hooves bearing down on them once more. Ward grabbed Carman and with the child in her arms; he pushed them to the ground and away from the fire. The sound of rumbling hooves came closer, then through the campsite rode many braves overrunning everything in sight. Angry braves sounded their war cries then rode off into the moonlit night. Their chilling cries faded far into the distance. The night become still, except for the burning wagon.

With a blanket wrapped around the child, Carman held her tightly. At the beginning of the onslaught by the screaming braves, the child quickly quieted down and lay still in Carman's arms.

Ward jumped to his feet and rushed over to where Carman was standing. "Are you all right, and how about the child?"

"I don't think I'll ever be all right, Ward, ever."

Ward slipped his arm around her and held her tightly. "We're going back and join the wagon train, Carman."

"We have nothing to travel with. No food, no clothing, nothing."

"We have each other don't we?" said Ward.

Carman looked up, "Are you asking me to marry you?"

"I didn't think so, but maybe it did sound like it," replied Ward, with some doubt in his voice.

Carman smiled. "It was close enough and you're right; we do have each other and the child."

Ward continued to carry water until there were no longer flames, flames that had nearly consumed Carman's wagon. After resting for a short time, they picked through the hot coals looking for anything that could be saved.

They both were covered with soot after trying to save some of Carman's belongings buried in the rubble. "Well, how did we do?" asked Ward.

With sweat pouring down her face, Carman placed the back of her hand to her brow and answered Ward. "We have a few tins, some flour and dried meat and that's about all."

"Do you like rabbit?" asked Ward.

"I sure do."

"Maybe we'll have a lot of that during the rest of our trip."

"That suits me and I'm sure the child will be satisfied with it."

Ward looked at Carman and smiled, "Would you like to bathe in the river? At least you'll be clean even though your clothes will still be soiled."

"Soiled?" laughed Carman. "They're down right dirty."

"I am glad you can laugh," smiled Ward. "You know I did make a big mistake thinking we could find a place for the child."

"Your heart was in the right place, Ward; I can see you are not a selfish person."

"Thank you, Carman, I try not to be. Now," continued Ward, "why don't you go wash or bathe if you wish. I'll watch over you, and if you need me just call out."

"May I take the blanket from your bedroll?" asked Carman.

"Well, certainly," replied Ward, hurriedly jerking the blanket from his roll and handing it to her.

The moon was full and bright. Carman's shadow walked ahead of her on her way to the river. The water was cold, but still it was refreshing and she was able to wash away a goodly amount of dirt. Above all it felt good to her to wash her hair and comb it out.

Ward was becoming concerned about her when she called out to him. He shouldered his rifle and ran frantically toward the river. Arriving, he was met by Carman wrapped in his blanket. "Yes, what is it and where's the child?"

"She's right here asleep by my clothes. I'm all right."

"I thought I told you to call me if you needed me."

"That's right you did."

"Well then?"

Carman walked up to Ward. "I do need you."

"What for?"

She let the blanket slip from her shoulders. "What are you doing?" exclaimed Ward, swallowing hard.

"I said I need you, Ward," she responded, tipping her head back and letting her hair hang between her shoulder blades.

"I don't know about this, Carman."

"I do, Ward. I have needed you ever since the second

day I saw you."

"But we still could be in danger out here."

"We were cautious before and look what it got us. I don't think there is much more that could happen tonight unless I become disappointed. You wouldn't want to do that would you?"

"I just don't know, Carman."

"I'll sit here on the blanket with the child while you bathe and then you can come back to me. I'll be ready."

Ward, frustrated, stepped to the river bank then into the water where he bathed. Returning to Carman, he found her sitting with the child in the center of the blanket. "Your body is so strong, Ward."

"I tell you, Carman, I don't know about this."

She reached for Ward's hand. A time of love began after which Carman made Ward promise it would not be the last.

"Things are so uncertain, Carman."

"Ward, all I'm asking you is tell me this will not be the last time—is that too much to ask?"

Ward brought her to him and kissed her. "No, Carman, that's not too much to ask and I promise this will not be the last time."

"Oh, Ward, thank you for saying that. Now, no matter what happens I can face it."

"This is important to you, isn't it?"

"You don't know, Ward; you just don't know."

Time passed swiftly while they lay in each others arms. Daylight had crept in. It was the beginning of a new day, and Carman could only hope it would be the beginning of a new life. Carman rolled over and looked at the child sound asleep on the edge of the blanket. "I guess she's ours."

"Maybe this night was meant to be. It has made us both realize a lot of things about ourselves and others," said Ward.

"That was nice, and so true."

Ward rolled over and got to his feet. "I'll go get the horses around and you can come back when you are ready."

Carman jumped to her feet and pressed her body to Ward's. "It was wonderful. I'll be with you in just a few minutes."

"If you don't mind me saying so, you have a beautiful

body, just beautiful."

"You know how to a make woman feel like a woman, don't you?"

"I swear, I don't tell everyone that."

"Somehow I believe you, Ward."

Ward kissed her and held her tightly. After their caress, he returned to the burned out wagon. He was missing his canteen and was hoping he might find it after the heat had subsided.

"What are you looking for?" asked Carman, returning from the river looking beautiful and content.

"My canteen."

"It's over here. It was one of the first things I recovered. It was on the ground and didn't appear to have been burned at all."

"Thank the Lord for that. We need our water," said Ward, shaking his head in disbelief that they had lost almost everything.

"I want to feed the child before we leave," said Carman, brushing the hair out of her eyes.

"What do we have for her?"

"I did save some flour, so I'll feed her that."

While Carman was feeding the child, Ward freed her horses from the tree to which they were tied. By hooking the tugs to their hames, he had them harnessed so that if necessary they could run.

After Carman finished feeding the child, she joined Ward who was still preparing the horses to leave.

"Which one of these horses do you want to ride?" asked Ward.

"The one with the star in the middle of his forehead. He has been ridden before, but I don't believe the others have."

Ward stripped the harness from the horse, rolled it up and tied it to the back of one of the others.

"Why are we carrying the extra harness?" asked Carman, looking on while Ward worked.

"Maybe one of the others in the wagon train will need a harness somewhere along the way."

"That's true," she replied, reaching down and taking the child in her arms. "Did you ever see a child react the way she did during the raid?"

"These children must be born with an instinct that comes into play when they encounter danger," reasoned Ward.

"Do I have time to look around the wagon one last time? There were some things in there that I wished I hadn't lost," said Carman. A forlorn look came over her face with her question.

"You go right ahead,"

Carman and the child returned to the burned out wagon while Ward removed his saddle and placed it on the back of Carman's horse. After he made some adjustments, his saddle fit Carman's horse perfectly.

Ward watched Carman from where he stood and shook his head in sadness. She walked with her head down, moving the ashes around with her foot. It was daylight and time to go. However, just before Ward was about to call to Carman, she shrieked. Ward ran to her side. "What is it?"

"The broach, I found the broach my grandmother gave me years ago," she shouted, clutching the piece in her hand. The chain hung loose between her fingers.

"Is that what you were looking for?" asked Ward, smiling back at Carman.

"Yes! Yes!" still clutching the broach and pressing it to her chest.

"This means a great deal to you."

"Oh, yes, she was the finest woman that ever took a breath. I loved her then and still do with all my heart."

"She really made an impact on your life, didn't she?"

"She was my strength when I needed strength. She was my joy when I needed to be happy."

"You were very lucky, Carman, to have had someone in your life that you feel this strongly about. Most people live a lifetime without knowing such love."

"And that is just what it is."

"May I ask you something?"

"Why, yes."

"Was she your mother or grandmother?"

Carman's face lost its smile."Yes, Ward that's just the way it was."

"You look sad, Carman. I shouldn't have ask you that."

"Oh, yes, it's all right. My mother fell on hard times and was not able to take care of me."

"I'm sorry, Carman. I'm sure she loved you."

"Not really, Ward. She made her own hard times. There was no place for me in the life she wanted to lead, so she left me."

Ward reached out for Carman. "No, Ward, please. I don't want anyone to feel sorry for me. What would I have been had I remained with my mother? You see, I don't really care about her for I don't know her. How can one long for a stranger?"

"You're a very strong person."

Carman, looking down at the broach laying in the palm of her hand, said, "We can leave now, Ward. This will give me the strength I need."

"I thought I was your strength?"

"You are, Ward, but I think you know what I mean."

"Yes, I know."

The weary child reached up and took Carman by the hand. Carman dropped to her knees, caressed the child and wept.

Ward looking on saw a tear trickle down the child's face and drop on Carman's shoulder. "She's crying with you, Carman, so hold her tightly. She doesn't know what's being said, yet she feels your sadness."

After Carman collected herself, she pushed back and looked at the child's tear soaked face. With a handkerchief she brushed away the tears from the child's face and then from her own. In return the child threw her arms around Carman's neck and hugged her. That was more than Ward could take, he turned quickly and walked away. "When you're ready, I'll be with the horses."

Carman smiled slightly and whispered, "He is a good man; I can't let him go."

After a short time, Ward heard a shuffling behind him. He turned. Carman and the child were near. She smiled at him. "I guess we're ready."

"You mount first," said Ward. "I'll hand you the child once you're set."

"Ward," exclaimed Carman. "This is your saddle; you can't do this."

"Yes, it is my saddle and yes, I can do it, so you get yourself up there on that horse."

Carman reached up and kissed Ward. "I guess my grandmother wasn't the only wonderful person in the world."

Placing his hands around her waist Ward helped her onto her horse. "Would you like to take him for a short ride? He's not used to being ridden, so you might want to take control and let him know it."

Carman spurred her horse on and rode hard over the plains for a short distance then returned. "There will be no problem here; he feels good under me."

Ward handed Carman the child, then gave her a small blanket to place between the saddle and the child. "That's nice of you, Ward. I know she can't tell you, but if she could she would thank you."

Ward patted Carman's boot and smiled up at her.

Carman scowled then looked at Ward with questioning eyes. "Where did you get this blanket?"

"I picked it up near where her mother lay. I thought it would give her some of the sights and smell of her natural surroundings."

"That should help her some when she wakes up in a totally new setting."

"I thought so."

Ward smiled back at Carman once more. "We should be going. We have a hard trip ahead of us."

Carman reached down and touched Ward on the shoulder. "Do you realize this child is alone in the world."

"She has us."

Shaking her head yes, Carman came back, "But what if later on she refuses to accept us?"

"Then we would have to let her go, if she was old enough to know what she really wanted."

"That makes me ill."

"Aren't you getting a little ahead of yourself?"

"Yes, I guess I am," sighed Carman, touching the child's soft cheek.

Ward saw a woman's love for a child deep in Carman's eyes as he turned and walked back to where the horses were tied.

"Do you think the Indians that attacked last night will come for us this morning?" called out Carman.

"I don't know, but I don't think we should stay here and wait," said Ward mounting his horse.

With Ward leading two of Carman's horses and Carman leading the remaining one, they struck out for the wagon train.

A breeze blowing in from over the mountain range to the west was cool, a welcome relief from the hot days they had been experiencing for the last few weeks.

While humming a lullaby, Carman looked at the world through eyes of love. Riding ahead of her was a man she never dreamed of knowing and in her arms a loving child.

The night before had been the most ugly time of her life. Wolves stalking her and Ward like wild animals themselves. Indians with vengeance in their hearts came and destroyed nearly everything she owned. Carman was sure they had suffered for those killings carried out by the cavalry against an Indian camp of the old men, women and children. In her heart she could not fault the braves for revenging their loses using any means they had.

After the exhausted child dozed off in Carman's arms, Carman leaned back in her saddle and looked beyond Ward riding ahead. There she saw a country rough and beautiful. Lazy white clouds moved slowly over the majestic peaks, part of a mountain range to the right.

Suddenly, something caught Carman's eye. She looked high in the sky and circling gracefully overhead was a giant bald eagle. From where she was sitting she saw no movement of his wings, but still he soared with all the grace that nature had bestowed upon him.

Carman adjusted the blanket Ward had given her so as to keep the morning sun out of her eyes.

With the child asleep in her arms Carman rode up alongside Ward.

"How's she doing?" asked Ward, glancing over at Carman with admiring eyes.

"She's asleep."

✢✢✢✢✢✢✢ CHAPTER TWELVE ✢✢✢✢✢✢✢

IN THE MEANTIME, Mr. Hineburg had taken his place out on the point as Hawk's scout.

During their preparation before leaving that morning, a young boy from one of the wagons frightened a skittish horse and was kicked severely in the side. His mother, Hannah Strong, remained in the wagon with the boy trying to keep him comfortable. It was nearly 3:00 p.m. when the boy took what Mrs. Strong thought was his last breath. She leaped to the ground and ran frantically over to Emily's wagon, waving her hand and shouting. Emily, seeing Mrs. Strong's face, stopped her teams and jumped to the ground.

"I think my boy is dead," cried out Mrs. Strong.

Emily shouted to one of the men riding by, "Go get Hawk at once." With the man underway, Emily hurried back to the Strong's wagon, jumped in through the back and was at the boy's side.

"Is he dead?" asked Mrs. Strong.

Emily looked up through a scowl, "No, but he's in a coma. All we can do is wait and see if he'll come out of it."

"I can't lose him, Emily. I just can't."

The opening at the rear of the wagon flew open. It was Mrs. Strong's husband, Sam. "What is it, Hannah?"

With her face buried in her hands, Hannah wept. "I'm afraid we're not going to have him much longer."

Sam sat next to her and took her by the hand. "We must have faith, Hannah; we must."

"I know, Sam, but we can't lose him."

Hawk's booming voice shattered the stillness around the Strong's wagon. "What is it, Emily? We can't be stopping for every little thing that goes on here."

Emily, like a wet hen, was out of the wagon and standing with her finger in Hawk's face. "Now you listen to me, Hawk. The Strong boy is on the edge of life and death and by damn you are going to hold this train up. The only one that would complain would be you. Now if you can't help in this situation then get the hell out of here and let us try to save the boy. Is that asking too much?"

"I didn't know, Emily," said Hawk quietly.

"That's just the way you are. You start running off at the mouth and bulling your way through everything before you know what is going on, now you get."

Emily returned to the wagon, leaving more concerned settlers standing outside.

Hawk looked into their faces and said, "How was I to know?"

From the back row of the gathering came a deep and booming voice, "Just listen to what someone has to say would be a start."

Hawk dropped his head. "I guess you're right."

Nearly an hour had passed when a loud cry went up near the end of the wagon train. It was coming from the Strong's wagon. A knot came to Hawk's throat and he choked. Slowly he made his way to the Strong's wagon and met with Emily who was out and on the ground. "Couldn't save the lad?"

"No, Hawk. He was too young to have his life snuffed out and he was such a nice young man."

"They have a younger boy and a girl left, don't they?"

"Yes, Hawk, but—"

"Emily, don't blow up again. I was just inquiring or maybe I was looking for something to say."

"It's all right, Hawk, I understand," she replied, reaching out and touching Hawk's rough red hand.

"Thank you, Emily."

Emily smiled slightly and was about to walk away when Hawk said, "We'll have the burial in a couple of hours, so would you tell the Strongs for me? Now I'm going out and bring Mr. Hineburg in off the point." With that said, Hawk hurried to his horse, mounted and thundered away in search of Mr. Hineburg.

Emily couldn't help but to smile to herself, realizing she

had been left with the task of making the arrangements and trying to console the family after their loss. Emily, a mite of a woman in stature, but a monument of a person, joined the Strong family, grieving in disbelief. "Hannah," said Emily, placing her hand on Hannah's shoulder.

Hannah looked up through swollen eyes. "I think I know what you are going to say."

"We must bury your son and go on."

"I don't know that I want to go on."

Mr. Strong joined Emily and spoke softly to his wife, "Yes, Hannah, this is our tragedy, and we'll carry it with us the rest of our lives. However, we must remember that those who are in the train have lives and dreams ahead of them and we can not hold them up. We have dreams for ourselves and our children that we must and will realize when we arrive at our destination."

"I know that, Sam, and it's unfair of me to be so selfish."

Emily grasped Hannah's hand. "You're not selfish, Hannah; you're a mother and we all understand. However, your husband is right; we must carry on."

A shadow passed over Emily's shoulder. She looked up and standing there was Mrs. Worton. "May I help?"

"Would you?" replied Emily, pushing herself up on her feet and turning to Sam Strong. With Emily's hand in his, they walked to the rear of the wagon.

"Could we have the same funeral as we had for Mr. Worton?" asked Sam, wiping a tear from his cheek.

"I'm afraid not. As you remember, it was Carman who said the words over Mr. Worton, but she is no longer with us."

"That's right, I had forgotten," Sam paused. "Then would you say a few words, Emily?"

"Oh, my land no. I'm not fit to be holding the Bible, let alone read from it."

"Maybe you don't give yourself enough credit, but I'm telling you one thing we all do. I think the Lord would be mighty proud to have you read from the good book."

"You think so?"

"Yes, Emily, I do."

"And so do I," said one of the women who had just left Mrs. Strong.

"Well, if you don't think it would be hypocritical of me."

"Please do this for me, Emily," was Sam's choking response.

During the time Emily was talking with the family, the men of the wagon train had dug a grave near a small green shrub just off the trail.

"I must get my Bible," said Emily, with shaking hands.

"Here," said one of the women, "Would you use mine?" Emily reached for the Bible and was about to speak when the lady continued, "I have marked a couple of pages that you might want to read from."

"Oh, thank you," exclaimed Emily, clutching the Bible tightly in her hand.

"I guess we're ready," said Sam, coming up behind Emily with Hannah at his side and their two other children walking behind.

Emily's knees, weak, nearly buckled out from under her when she stepped up to the open grave holding the boy wrapped in a brightly colored crazy quilt.

Looking into the glazed eyes of the family and the others who stood at the grave, Emily began to read.

During the funeral, Hawk and Mr. Hineburg rode into camp and quietly joined the others.

After the service was over, everyone left, leaving Emily still staring at the small boy laying before her. "Come, Emily," said Hawk. "You've done all you can do and you did a fine job, just a fine job."

"You know, Hawk, it felt so good holding the Bible in my hands once more."

"That's good, Emily; now we must go."

"I'm not going until I tell you something."

"All right, Emily. What is it?"

"You may not believe this, but I went to Sunday school and church when I was a little girl."

"Why shouldn't I believe it, Emily?"

"Then you do believe me?"

"Well, of course I do. You are a good person and we all know that. The only person on the train that puts you down is yourself."

Emily looked away from the grave and into Hawk's softened eyes. "You think so?"

"Well, yes, you're not a bad person."

"How about us and, and—"

"Now Emily, let's not get into that. If we do, your conscience will eat you up."

"Yes, and that would take away your pleasures."

"That wasn't fair, Emily."

"Don't expect it was and I don't see how we are going to change after all these years. I sure wish you would make a honest woman out of me someday." Emily closed the Bible and walked with Hawk over to where Sam and Hannah Strong were standing near their wagon.

Hawk reached out and shook hands with Sam. "A hard pill to take, but I guess none of us knew when we left Hannibal if we would make it to the West Coast or not."

"I know, Hawk," replied Sam. "The family and I had a long talk about taking this trip. I might say we talked about something like this happening. As you know, Hawk, you think bad luck only falls on the other man."

"There's something to be said about that," agreed Hawk, releasing Sam's hand.

"We're ready whenever you are, Hawk." said Sam.

Hawk returned to the head of the column; there he spoke a few words to Mr. Hineburg before he struck out for the point then shouted, "Move 'em out! We're heading for California." Everyone scurried to their wagons and readied them for another day of facing the unknown.

Hannah, with her children at her side, walked over to the grave once more, took a deep breath, then left with a heavy heart buried deep in her chest.

Slowly the train moved on west. Just before the grave was out of sight, Sam Strong grabbed Hannah to keep her from wilting like a weed in the sun. "Hannah, we must go on; if not for us, the children."

"I know, Sam, but there is a part of me we left back there."

"And of me, Hannah, this is not easy for either one of us."

It was staying light longer than it had the day they left Hannibal and Hawk had been taking advantage of the daylight to get a few more miles in before he camped. However, realizing the Strongs had almost more than they could handle for one lifetime, Hawk rode the full length of the train. "All right, folks, we'll be making camp just beyond that wall of granite dead ahead. There's a watering hole there where we can water the livestock. It's no good for man, but I think we all have enough water for a few more days."

Sam, driving his team from alongside, had put Hannah in the wagon somewhere along the way. She was just too weak to go on by foot.

"How's it going, Sam?" shouted Hawk, on his way toward the head of the train.

"As good as can be expected, I guess."

"I know."

"You think you do, Hawk?"

"Now let's not go into that. I've seen more graves dug along this trail than I'd like to talk about, so don't tell me I don't understand."

"Sorry, Hawk."

"That's all right."

The wagons were nearly in a circle when Leaky with his teams of mules and wagon came trudging in from the rear.

"How's everything back there?" shouted Hawk, riding up to Leaky.

"Quiet as all get out, but I can't remember eating as much dust as I have today."

"I know, Leaky," said Hawk. "This area is dry and we'll be in it for the next few days."

Approaching the water hole, Hawk shouted while waving his hands in the air, "Hold up everyone."

The wagon train groaned to a halt. "Leaky," shouted Hawk, "get yourself up here."

"Yes, what is it?"

"Look up there," said Hawk, pointing toward the water hole.

"Isn't that Mr. Hineburg on the ground?" asked Leaky.

"Yes, and we're going to find out what happened out there."

"I'll go," said Leaky.

"We'll go together," responded Hawk, waving for Strong to come forward.

Strong spurred his horse and was at Hawk's side. "What

is it?"

Hawk still staring in the direction of the water hole grunted, "I don't know yet, but while Leaky and I are gone, Strong, you're going to take charge of the train."

"Me?" exclaimed Strong.

"Your name is Strong, isn't it?"

"Well, yes."

"Then I mean you. Now if anyone asks what is going on, just tell them Leaky and I are scouting ahead. Do you hear me?"

"I'll do my best, Hawk."

"You'll do just fine; just don't alarm anyone."

"I won't."

"Oh, yes, Strong, get off your horse. I want Leaky to ride him while we're out there and you take care of Leaky's teams."

Strong's tone was that of resistance. "I don't know about that, Hawk."

"Well, by damn I do, now get down off that horse."

Reluctantly, Strong dropped to the ground and Leaky handed him the reins to the two teams of mules.

Scrambling into the saddle on Strong's horse, Leaky and Hawk thundered toward Mr. Hineburg who lay on the ground near the water hole. Upon arriving they found him up on one elbow. Hawk jumped to the ground and dropped to his knees at Mr. Hineburg's side. "What happened here?"

Mr. Hineburg with glazed eyes mumbled, "I don't know. My horse was drinking, then for no apparent reason he reared up, sending me out of the saddle and onto the ground. I guess I hit my head a pretty good clip."

"Just take it easy," said Hawk. "We'll talk about what happened when you collect you wits."

Leaky, seeing Mr. Hineburg's horse standing near a scrub tree, walked slowly toward the animal. After several tries to get near the horse, Leaky was able to catch the reins and lead the horse back to where Mr. Hineburg was standing on weakened legs with the help of Hawk.

"For awhile I didn't think he was going to let me get near him," said Leaky. "He's still pretty skittish."

Confused, Hineburg muttered, "I don't know what happened. I had stopped to look over the water hole when he reared up and sent me off backwards. When I hit the ground, I thought he was coming over onto me."

"You saw or heard nothing— is that right?" asked Hawk, keeping a keen eye on everything around him.

"Nothing, it was as quiet as it had been all day. Matter of fact, it was a deadly calm."

Hawk, pushing his hat forward, took a deep breath. "This is a strange one."

"I've got a funny feeling about this place myself, Hawk," chirped in Leaky.

Hawk with his hand still on Mr. Hineburg's shoulder spoke up, "You feel like riding?"

"I think so."

"All right, you ride back with Leaky and I'm going on ahead."

"I'll go with you, Hawk."

"No, Leaky, you go with Mr. Hineburg. Furthermore, I don't think there should be anything said about this back at camp," said Hawk, holding his reins high, ready to ride out.

"I think they have a right to know," disagreed Mr. Hineburg.

"There's nothing for them to know. If I had something to tell them that would be different, but to let everyone's imagination run wild would be unfair, don't you think?

"You have a point and I trust your judgment," concurred Mr. Hineburg.

"All right, you and Leaky mount up and get back to camp. Try not to get yourselves trapped into a conversation that would upset someone. Do you hear me?"

Both Leaky and Mr. Hineburg assured Hawk they would go on as if nothing had happened and leave the questions to him.

Hawk smiled, "Now you got it."

Leaky and Mr. Hineburg waited until Hawk disappeared, then returned to camp.

"What's going on out there and where is Hawk?" inquired Emily, standing with her hands on her hips.

"Nothing, ma'am," replied Mr. Hineburg. "Hawk just wanted to ride on ahead, that's all."

"Why did he go out there in the first place?" she went on.

"Ma'am," said Mr. Hineburg, removing his hat, "how

does anyone know what Hawk is going to do from one minute to the next."

"I guess you're right. I've been around him for a long time and sometimes he doesn't know why he does things," chuckled Emily, turning away and strolling in the direction of her wagon.

Leaky took a deep breath and smiled through his tobacco stained teeth. "You sure handled that all right. Usually that woman can dig a thought out of your head if she sets her mind to it."

The camp was buzzing, just knowing that Hawk didn't return with Leaky and Mr. Hineburg. Strong too, seemed to be concerned when he spoke with the two men. "Is this serious, gentlemen?"

"Nothing wrong with Hawk taking a ride on ahead of the train is there? The way I see it, that's his job," responded Mr. Hineburg.

"Well, no, but when he turned the train over to me he did show some concern."

Leaky, holding himself from becoming angry, took a deep breath. "Strong, Hawk can do any damn thing he wants to do and he can run this train anyway he wants to and there ain't none of us got a thing to say about it."

"I realize that, Leaky, but seeing the look on Hawk's face when he rode out of here has got me concerned."

"Then why in the hell don't you wait until he gets back. I'd like to see how you come on to him about this."

Mr. Hineburg smiled. "Me too."

A scowl came over Strong's face. "You want to give me my horse back, Leaky?"

Leaky laughed out loud. "It's feeling real good being on a horse again. Mighty fine animal you have here." Leaky jumped to the ground and turned the reins over to Strong. "Where's my mules?"

Strong pointed to the back of the train. "They're tied to the last wagon."

It was nearly an hour before Hawk rode back and ordered the wagons to move out.

Approaching the water hole, Hawk rode to the lead wagon. "Stay a good distance away from the water hole. We don't want all those varmints coming into camp that might visit the water hole during the night." The settlers waved and started forming the nightly circle.

Emily joined Hawk sitting high in his saddle watching the wagons being maneuvered into place. "Where do you think Ward and Carman are tonight?"

"Don't know, Emily, but I'll tell you this much, I hated to see them ride out of here."

"Do you know something they should have known?"

"All I can say is that the territory they're riding into is a hotbed."

"Why didn't you tell them?"

"I did tell Ward, but he and Carman were so darn cocked and primed, ready to get that Indian Child back in the hands of her kind that he wouldn't listen to me."

"And don't you think the way he feels about Carman had something to do with it?"

"Sure I do," muttered Hawk. "That's the way it is with all good men."

"What do you mean by that?" asked Emily, placing her hands on her hips and tapping the toe of her boot on the ground.

"Just what I said. You get a man all moon-eyed over a woman and he can't see his hand in front of his face."

"Well, you sure don't have to worry about seeing anything beyond your nose when it comes to women."

"That's not fair, Emily."

"Well, it is. If I wasn't here talking to you, you wouldn't know I was in camp," she snapped. A bit of sadness crossed her face.

"Now, Emily. I know you're talking about us and I don't think that's right."

"If the shoe fits, Hawkshaw, you can wear it."

Hawk dismounted and walked over to where Emily was standing. "You mind if I come to your wagon tonight for supper?"

Emily, all puffed up, said, "I expect you can; I've got to eat anyway."

Hawk's smile widened and his eyes twinkled. "I'll be there in a short time."

"Now you look here, Hawk. I can see it in your eyes. You're a wantin' to have more than supper with me tonight;

it's all over your face."

"Why did you go and say a thing like that, Emily?"

"'Cause it's true, that's why."

"Can I still come over for supper?"

"Well, of course you can, Hawk. You know I've always got enough on the fire for the both of us," Emily smiled to herself then with her skirt a swaying, she swaggered off toward her wagon.

Hawk watched Emily with admiring eyes until she was out of sight then rode over to talk with Leaky. "How was everything at the rear today?"

"Quiet."

"That's the way we like it, Leaky. Now for tomorrow I want you up front."

"Up front?"

"That's what I said."

"You expecting trouble?"

"Not the way you might think. There's a nasty river up there ahead. We usually lose a few head of cattle and the wagons have a hell of a time getting across."

"Why don't we cross where it's not so fast?"

"Because there's not another place to cross within a hundred miles in either direction. Does that answer your question?"

"Yes, Hawk. I was only asking."

"All right, but I think I'll want you to drive Mrs. Worton's wagon across the river for her. You might have to help some of the others; I don't know how good some of these men might be in a situation like this."

"How do you know I'll be any good?" asked Leaky.

"I've watched you, and I think you can handle a team in just about any situation."

Leaky puffed up like a bullfrog on a lily pad. "I might just have to unhitch some of these teams of horses and take the wagons across with my mules. I know what they can do and damn if I don't reckon they can think when it comes to something like this, where a horse gets all rattled."

"Whatever we have to do, Leaky. I know I can depend on you."

"You know, Hawk, you're not such a bad fellow after all."

"Did you think I was?"

"No, no, I didn't mean it that way, Hawk. You know what I mean?"

"Yes, Leaky, I know what you mean."

Hawk then made it a point to check in with every wagon telling the settlers they would be faced with some hard going the following day and that they should make sure everything in their wagons was secure.

"What are we faced with?" asked one of the men.

"There's a nasty river ahead and it could take its toll on wagons and animals. I've never gotten through that river without losing more than we can afford. Now try to get all the rest you can, for tomorrow is going to be a big day for all of us."

After making the rounds, Hawk joined Emily for dinner, then turned in early.

CHAPTER THIRTEEN

IN THE MEANTIME, WARD AND CARMAN had made it back as far as the wagon trail by dusk. They had hoped to join Hawk and the wagon train before sundown, but with the Indian Child in Carman's arms it was impossible to ride as hard as Ward had planned.

After feeding the child, Ward and Carman ate from what little they had of dried beef then stretched out on the ground near a small fire Ward had started. The weary child laid on one of Ward's blankets sound asleep.

Carman's glances at the child were filled with love. "You know, Ward, she is a pretty little thing, isn't she?"

"Well, yes."

"Don't you think so?"

"Yes, Carman, I do."

"Why did you say it that way?"

"I guess it's just that I think she should be back with her own people."

"That doesn't change the fact that she is a lovely child," countered Carman.

"Oh, no, I didn't mean anything by that remark."

"I guess I understand. You're still looking ahead, aren't you?"

"That's right, Carman. It appears that it's like taking a fawn away from her mother."

"I suppose you could say that," agreed Carman, laying down beside the child.

It was dark and Ward was still sitting by the fire half awake and half asleep when the horses became uneasy. Ward sprang to his feet and grabbed his rifle. Quietly he walked to where the horses were tied. From the light of the fire and into the bright moonlight, a shadow moved in the distance. It was either an animal or someone crouched. The horses tugged at their reins and stomped their feet nervously. Ward held his breath and soon discovered it was a wolf prowling in the darkness. After staying with the horses and seeing them settle down, Ward joined Carman and turned in for the night, keeping his rifle across his chest.

The night was a fitful time for Ward. Half-dozing and half-awake, he welcomed the first sign of dawn. The fire was but a bed of coals and beside it was Carman curled up in a ball with the child held tightly to her.

"Carman," whispered Ward.

"Yes, what is it?"

"It's time for us to leave."

"So soon?"

"Yes, Carman. I'm hoping we can be with the wagon train by this afternoon if we get a jump on them this morning."

"I must feed the child."

"I know, but let's hurry."

"Here, hold her while I get her some flour."

Ward took the child in his arms and held her. "She doesn't seem frightened of us, does she?"

"Not a bit," replied Carman. "Did you think she would be?"

"I sure did. We're very different to her, but I think she feels like she's in her mother's arms when you're holding her."

Carman smiled. "She's not fussing with you holding her."

"I see that," replied Ward, looking into the child's shinning face.

After the child was fed, Ward, Carman and the child mounted then headed out, following the trail used by Hawk and the wagon train.

The trail was familiar to Ward for he had rode the point while the wagon train moved west over that very trail.

They rode hard and just before noon, Ward raised his hand and pointed straight ahead.

"I don't understand," shouted Carman, riding up alongside Ward.

"See that cloud of dust just ahead?"

"Yes, what does it mean?"

"That means we are just that far from Hawk and the wagon train."

A wide smile graced Carman's face, "That sounds good to me." Carman looked into the child's face. "You can have something beside flour and water, little one."

They rode hard and soon they found themselves coming up onto the wagon train dead ahead. Carman nearly wept with joy for she was back with the friends she had made and she still had the Indian Child.

Their horses seemed to sense the arrival and pounded their hooves to the rocky terrain. Thundering by the last wagon, they rode on up to where Hawk was riding several wagon lengths beyond the column. Hawk whirled his horse around and threw his hat in the air. "Damn, if I'm not glad to see you right about now!"

"We're glad to be back, Hawk," said Ward.

Carman with a broad smile joined the two men in a reunion that meant a lot to each of them.

"Where's Leaky?" asked Ward. "I didn't see him at the tail end."

"He's leading the train today."

"You let Leaky take the lead?"

"You bet I did. We have a dangerous river crossing up ahead and I think he's the man to take some of these wagons across."

Hawk filled Ward in on the river and also told him he had let the settlers know what they were up against the night before.

Ward glanced back at Carman. "I guess that's the way to do it. Let them know so they can prepare for whatever comes along."

"This is a gritty bunch we have here, Ward. Can't remember when I had one like it," said Hawk proudly. Hawk hesitated. "Where's your wagon, Ward?"

"We lost it in a Indian raid."

"You what?"

"That's right, so what you see here is all we have."

"That don't worry me, but are you two all right?"

Carman spoke up sharply. "We three are just fine, now."

"I'm sorry, Carman," said Hawk, removing his hat and

brushing his hair back.

"That's all right, Hawk," responded Carman, stroking the child's arm.

"Well, tell me what happened," insisted Hawk.

"That can come later," said Ward. "Now, do you want me to take the point?"

"Not today, Ward. Mr. Hineburg has been out there and I wouldn't want to replace him right now. Matter of fact, he is doing a real good job."

"He needs this to keep his mind off his wife. I wouldn't want to interfere with that," agreed Ward.

"Thought you might understand."

"How far are we from the river you're talking about, Hawk?" inquired Ward, patting his horse on the neck.

"Mr. Hineburg should be there in an hour or so."

Ward frowned, "Still can't see Leaky taking the lead."

"I think he has the most experience of anyone in this train when it comes to handling a team. And I guess I'll have to eat my words, but his mules may be our answer to getting some of these wagons across our challenge ahead."

Ward nodded. "Think I'll go out there and find him. We need a wagon to lead Carman's three horses. I hope there will be enough room for her and the child to sleep at night."

"Go ahead," replied Hawk.

Carman looked up and down the train and then smiled. "Oh, there she is."

"Who's that?" inquired Hawk.

"Emily."

"Why don't you go see her. I know she'll be glad to see you back and if I'm any judge, she'll want to hold the child for awhile."

While Carman was with Emily, Ward, with Carman's three horses rode out to see Leaky. "How you coming, Leaky?"

Leaky turned and came straight up in the seat, "What you doing back here, Ward?"

"It's a long story and I'll tell you about it sometime. But what I'm here for is to see if there is room enough for Carman and the child to sleep in your wagon. We lost everything while we were gone."

"I expect so. It might be a little tight back there, but I

think we can make do."

"I'm also going to tie Carman's three horses to the back of your wagon."

"What happened to the fourth one?" asked Leaky, turning in his seat.

"She's riding that one."

"Well, heck yes," giggled Leaky.

After tying the horses to Leaky's wagon, Ward returned to Hawk. "What can I do, Hawk?"

"Nothing right now, but don't worry, it won't be long before we'll all have our hands full."

The wagon train rolled on with anxious settlers dreading the upcoming crossing Hawk had told them about.

Ward, now riding alongside Hawk, strained his eyes. "I think there's a rider bearing down on us, Hawk."

"Sure wish I had your young eyes again. What's he riding?"

"Can't tell yet, but Leaky has stopped his team."

"Come on Ward, let's go see."

Hawk with Ward, rode hard to meet the rider and found it to be Mr. Hineburg. "What's up?" shouted Hawk.

Mr. Hineburg pulled up and stopped, followed by a cloud of dust. "The river is on the other side of that gorge. You're right; it's a torrent."

"White water?" asked Hawk, staring in the direction of the gorge.

"You bet there is and plenty of it."

"A mean one?" asked Ward.

Hawk still looking on replied, "Yes, it's a mean one."

"What can I do?" asked Ward.

"Go on back and have Leaky bring the train up. I'll meet you at the river." With that, Hawk and Mr. Hineburg rode on down the trail while Ward returned to the wagon train.

"Bring 'em along, Leaky. Our next stop is the river."

"How's it look?"

"Don't know. I didn't get that far."

Leaky stood up and motioned for the wagons to move out.

Ward then rode on back to see how Carman and the child was doing and found them in Emily's wagon. "How you doing in there, Carman?"

Carman looked out between the rear flaps. "She's asleep. The poor little thing is all tuckered out."

"How about you?"

"I'm holding up all right."

Ward smiled warmly. "You take care and I'll see you at the river crossing."

"You be careful, Ward," she said, returning Ward's smile.

The wagons groaned out the next few miles and soon they were breaking over the crest of a hill. Straight ahead was the angry river. The settlers looked on, wondering if it would be their livestock or wagon that would not make it across the churning waters.

Hawk with Ward at his side looked over the area and found a gentle slope leading to the water's edge. The white water churned with a vengeance as it moved swiftly downstream.

"She's sure on a rampage this time," said Hawk, waving his hands to hold up the wagons.

"You said it was a nasty one and it sure is," agreed Ward, watching the concern on Hawk's face.

"Are we going to wait until she settles down?" asked Ward.

"Don't think so. By the looks of the head of water coming down, we'd be here for a month and that would depend on whether there was any more rain in the mountains."

"Do you think these people have the experience to take their units across to safety?" asked Ward, swinging his leg over his saddle and dropping to the ground.

"We're about to find out," replied Hawk. "Now that brings me to another thing."

"What's that?"

"How are you with a team?"

Ward looking up at Hawk said, "I handled my share during the war."

"Thought you were in the cavalry."

Ward pushed his hat to the back of his head. "When things got tough, we did anything we had to, to keep from getting ourselves killed."

"I knew you were good stock the first time I laid eyes on you, Ward. I've been wrong a few times, but I sure wasn't this time."

"I guess I'm suppose to thank you for your confidence, but maybe we should wait until we are across this angry piece of water."

"Well, let's see what we have to do." Hawk turned and walked over to Leaky's wagon. Placing his hand on Leaky's leg, Hawk said, "I want you to take your wagon across this river. I don't know what you're going to find out there in the middle; this fast moving current could have changed the river bottom. We won't know that until you're across."

Leaky swallowed hard, "That's if I make it."

"If you and those mules can't handle that river, there is no one on this side of the Mississippi that can."

"Compliments ain't gonna keep me alive, Hawk."

Hawk raised his voice, "Get that team in the water or I'll have Emily come up here and take them across for you."

Chewing hard on his tobacco, Leaky snapped back, "You are a nasty bastard, aren't you Hawk?"

"Are you going?" shouted Hawk, shaking his fist in Leaky's face.

Leaky gathered the reins in his hands, spit his tobacco juice over his shoulder and yelled, "All right, you mules, it looks like we got to show these horses how it's done."

"Wait a minute, Leaky," called out Ward.

"What now?" asked Hawk in a loud voice.

Ward ignored Hawk and handed Leaky one end of a small diameter rope. "Take this with you, Leaky. We may need it to pull a large rope across."

"What for?" growled Hawk.

Ward turned to Hawk, "This time you don't have anything to say about it."

Leaky tied the rope to his wagon and climbed back on. With a roll of the reins out over the mule's back and a click of his tongue, Leaky moved his teams to the water's edge.

By this time most of the settlers had gathered at the river bank to watch and see if Leaky would be able to ford the river.

The teams entered the river and were up to their bellies in churning water. With the water broadsiding the wagon, Leaky felt the wagon lift. He jumped to the upside, adding his weight.

Hawk looked on, moving his shoulders with every motion Leaky made. Suddenly the wagon came up off the bottom. The rear end swung around, leaving the wagon facing upstream. The mules stumbled along until one of them went down. Leaky with all his strength and his teeth clenched, leaped from his seat onto the back of the mule nearest to him. From there, he worked his way along the back of the slippery animal until he reached the hames. Setting himself, he jumped to the lead mule that was still standing. They were losing ground, but Leaky was not giving up. Hanging on to the hames with one hand, he pulled frantically on the reins of the mule still down in the raging water.

"Come on, you mangy mule, get up and get your feet on the ground." Leaky had left the mules back and was standing on the tugs. His face was strained as he bit at the air trying to get the animal onto his feet. "If you don't get up," shouted Leaky, "we're all going downstream!"

"Oh, my God," said Hawk under his breath, "he's going to get himself killed."

"No, Hawk, you will have killed him. You're paid to lead this wagon train, not watch someone else do the dangerous work for you."

Hawk whirled around. It was Emily looking at him with scorn.

Hawk glanced toward the river in time to see the down mule come up on his feet. Shouts of encouragement went up from the settlers standing ridged on the river bank.

Leaky, gasping for air, found the team's shoulder deep in the water. Straddling the lead mule that had remained on his feet, Leaky talked to him like a preacher on his knees. "Come on, mule, move—do you hear me? Move!" Finally the teams came together and stepped off in the direction of the west bank. The rear of the wagon still facing downstream turned slowly and came in behind the mules. With every cautious step they moved closer to the opposite side. Finally the first team struggled up onto dry land.

With Leaky and his teams safe on the other side, joy erupted. The settlers locked their arms together, dancing around and around.

Leaky jumped to the ground and while still hanging on

to one of the mule's collar, he reached into his back pocket and grabbed for his tobacco pouch. From the pouch he pulled out a wad of wet tobacco and pushed it into his mouth. After a couple of chews he looked back at Hawk and motioned for him to come across.

Hawk grabbed his hat and slammed it to the ground. "This ain't no game we're playing here, Leaky."

Leaky unable to hear over the roar of the water, just smiled back.

"He has a right to challenge you to come across, Hawk," said Emily.

"Damn it, Emily, I'm tired of hearing you take sides with everyone but me."

While Hawk and Emily were going at it, Ward tied a heavy rope to the small rope he had given to Leaky. He motioned for Leaky to pull it across.

Leaky wrapped the rope around the brake handle and drove his teams ahead. With one end of the large rope on Leaky's side he secured it to a pine tree some distance away from the water's edge.

With the rope in place, Leaky gave Ward a wave and stood back waiting for the next wagon to begin the crossing.

Hawk motioned for the next settler to pull his wagon up and prepare to enter the water.

After watching the current, Ward suggested, "Why don't we start across about five wagon lengths upstream."

"Now, what's this all about?" shouted Hawk, glaring at Ward.

"You see the raging water there where Leaky went across?"

Hawk nodded and continued to listen to Ward.

"The water is not as violent above and that might indicate the river bed is less rocky than where Leaky crossed."

Jim Carter driving the second wagon, moved upstream and entered the river. His teams were flighty, but Jim appeared to have them under control. Step by step they moved slowly toward the center of the river and a powerful current. The teams started to flounder. Carter snapped a whip out over them. The horses were in deep water by then, but it appeared the river bottom was less rocky than where Leaky had gone across.

Suddenly the current lifted the wagon and rolled it over on its side. Mrs. Carter and their two children were jerked around violently. Clinging to the braces that held the canvas top, the children wailed out loud. The dry, white canvas helped float the wagon, keeping it from rolling upside down. Carter called on his teams to give him all they had. The horses' eyes were fiery red and they pawed their way through the rushing water that threatened to knock their legs out from under them.

Leaky seeing what was happening, backed his wagon to the river bank. When Carter's wagon bogged down in still water, Leaky rushed into the river and with a chain, he pushed his way in between the teams. After fastening the chain to the wagon tongue he secured it to the back of his wagon. Leaky standing alongside the mules cracked a whip and shouted at the top of his voice. Carter, standing on the upside of the wagon also cracked a whip out over his teams.

With the help of Leaky's team, they dragged Carter's wagon, still on its side, out onto dry land. Mrs. Carter and the two children frightened almost beyond control, leaped from the wagon and lay face down on the ground. With her hands, Mrs. Carter dug into the good earth as if hanging on to the world. Jim Carter jumped from the wagon, rushed directly to his horses in an attempt to settle them down.

Leaky joined Mrs. Carter and her children. "Here, here, now. You're not going to fall off the world. Everyone is safe."

"Safe from the water," exclaimed Mrs. Carter, "but what is next for us? Are we ever going to make it or will we all be buried along the trail like the others?"

Leaky felt a hand on his shoulder and looked up. It was Jim Carter. "Would you take care of my teams for a minute? I think I'm needed here."

"Sure," replied Leaky, jumping to his feet and hurrying over to the horses. Still with red bloodshot eyes and hammering hooves, they quivered and tossed their heads.

It was hours before the last wagon was across the river. They had lost several head of cattle; however, everyone in the train had survived the ordeal.

Tears flowed while the settlers hugged each other and thanked the good Lord for helping them make it through one more hazard.

Ward and Emily assembled the settlers, so that Hawk could address them. Hawk, a bit humble said, "I had just told Ward before we started across the river that you were one of the best groups I've ever led to the West. Now after today there's not enough words to tell you what a hell of a job you did. I mean, men, women and children, every last one of you. Now, don't let this go to your head. We still have a ways to go and everyone is going to have to continue to carry their load, is that clear?"

"I want to thank Leaky for fording the river first," shouted one of them in the group.

"That was just one of the jobs that had to be done," countered Hawk.

"I don't think so," argued the man. "He risked his life to see what the angry waters had in store for us. I think we should at least thank him."

A round of applause went up, while Leaky stood with his chin on his chest as if he had done something he should be ashamed of.

"All right, all right. I think Leaky has had enough. Now, we're going to camp here for the night, so get your wagons in place."

Hawk walked over to where Leaky was standing and placed his hand on Leaky's shoulder. "That was a tough job I gave you and you handled it damn well. I appreciate it."

"Well, thank you, Hawk," Leaky paused, then said, "I don't hear anyone making fun of my mules."

Hawk grinned through his ragged beard. "I better not hear anyone say anything but good about your mules."

While Hawk and Leaky were talking, Ward joined Carman and the Indian Child at Leaky's wagon. "Are you and the child getting settled down some?"

Carman smiled up at Ward. "I want to thank you for taking Mrs. Worton's wagon across that terrible river."

"That's all right, Carman. By the time we got to her wagon we had learned a lot and the going was much easier."

"It was still difficult," replied Carman, reaching for

Ward's hand.

"Well, of course it was no picnic, but all that matters is that we're on this side safe and sound."

"Are we?" asked Carman.

"Well, yes," frowned Ward. "Why do you say that?"

"I guess I feel a little like Mrs. Carter. When is it ever going to stop?"

Ward held Carman's hand tightly in his and sighed, "When we get to California."

"Not before?"

"I don't know, Carman. Hawk hasn't been kind enough to tell me anything until we're on top of it."

"I think the rest feels the same way except for Emily; she knows this trail as well as Hawk."

"I know, but she doesn't dare to say a thing or he would come down on her." Ward stopped for a moment. "You know, Carman, Hawk is a good man for this. He's tough and that's what it takes. You never know what's coming up or when you could have some kind of a rebellion on the train."

"I suppose you're right, Ward. You couldn't have some pussyfoot out there catering to everyone's whim."

"Is the child asleep in Emily's wagon?"

"She just went to sleep this minute. The trip across the river took a lot out of her. Would you like to look in on her?"

"Sure."

Carman got to her feet and spread the rear flap slightly. Ward looked in on the child's shining face and smiled. "I don't know that any of us will sleep much tonight after crossing that river, but just look at her, she has no idea what could have happened to her...she trusts you, Carman."

"I know she does and that makes me feel so good."

"It should."

Ward started to walk away when he turned and looked back at Carman. "I don't know what we have left to eat in Leaky's wagon, but as soon as I'm through with whatever Hawk needs I'll check it out."

Carman smiled and laid over on one elbow, watching Ward's long stride as he walked away.

Approaching Hawk, Ward spoke up, "You going to circle the wagons tonight?"

"Not enough room, but we'll line them up in two rows

with the wagon tongues facing each other, so let's get the word out."

Moving out in opposite directions, Ward and Hawk instructed the settlers to line their wagons up according to Hawk's instructions.

While everyone was lining up, Ward located Leaky. "Do we have any dry food left in the wagon?"

"Don't know, but I'm having me one of those big trout I saw in the river."

"There's trout in there?" asked Ward, with a beaming smile on his face.

"You bet there is. I saw them when I was out of the water and in the water."

"Do you have anything to fish with?" inquired Ward.

"Sure do, I have a couple of fish hooks in my bag. I never thought I would have something anyone would want. All the belongings I have are wrapped up in an old cloth I carry with me. Makes me feel kind of good."

"It should, Leaky. Another thing, you did a real job this afternoon. No one on this wagon train is going to forget you."

"You're just saying that."

"No, I'm not. We all owe you a lot."

Leaky shook his head. "Well, I'll be."

"Now let's find one of those hooks and I'll catch us both some fish. What do you say?"

"That's all right with me, but I'd just as soon catch 'um."

Leaky rummaged around in the wagon and finally came up with a fishhook and a short piece of line. "Here, Ward, you go a fishing and as soon as I get this wagon lined up, I'll be over here to fish with you."

While fishing Ward felt a presence around him and looked up. It was Carman smiling down on him. "I thought you were going to see about something to eat."

With those words no more than said, Ward jerked his line and pulled out a large trout. While the fish was flopping on the ground, Ward grinned up at Carman. "You like trout?"

"Oh, yes, but I can't remember when I had it last."

Ward got to his feet and took Carman in his arms. "Well, you're going to have trout tonight."

"You going to cook it?" asked Carman.

"Sure I will, but don't blame me if it doesn't suit you."

"I won't, I promise."

Arm in arm they started to leave when they heard Leaky calling out, "Ward, I thought we were going to fish together?"

Ward waited until Leaky came to him. "I have a trout large enough for the three of us, so why don't we build a fire at your wagon and we can eat together. How does that sound?"

"You mean I get a chance to eat some of Carman's cooking?" giggled Leaky.

"No, you'll be eating my cooking."

"Yours?"

"Yes," replied Ward. "I have cooked a lot of fish and it will be good, even if I do have to say so myself. However, if you don't want to eat with us, you can catch your own."

"No, no," stammered Leaky. "I'll eat it even if it is your cooking."

Ward laughed. Carman with a grin on her face squeezed Ward's arm then said, "We'll see you shortly, right?"

"You bet. I don't want to miss out on a trout supper."

The settlers were a happy lot that night for they had gotten across the river without the loss of a life. There was a hum over the encampment as they laughed and joined in on fun among themselves.

CHAPTER FOURTEEN

WHILE WARD WAS PREPARING their fish for supper, Carman sat on a blanket watching the Indian Child play with a sock doll Carman had made for her. Carman could not keep her eyes off Ward as he went about cooking the fish. By the time they and Leaky had finished eating, Carman's eyes were soft and mellow. Ward had caught her glances and was nearly fevered inside.

Darkness was nearly upon them when Leaky left for a large fire burning in the center of the compound. With the child sound asleep on the blanket, Carman curled up in Ward's arms and wrapped them around her. A full moon appeared on the horizon. Word spread and everyone was out of their wagons, gazing at the crystal clear moon, like a galleon moving upward into the sky.

"That moon is doing something to me, Ward."

"I know; I feel it too."

"You want to go down by the river?"

"How about the child?

"I'll have Emily come sit with her, that is if she and Hawk are not feeling the same way we do."

Ward laughed quietly. "You know, Carman, I just can't see that."

"I must admit I can't either, but somehow everyone seems to have their mate out there somewhere."

"You're right about that. Now, were you going to see if Emily will stay with the little one?" asked Ward, looking into the peaceful face of the child who had just stretched and licked her lips without opening her eyes.

"Isn't she precious?" asked Carman, smiling down on the child, curled up in the nightie Carman had fashioned for her. With that, Carman left for Emily's wagon. There she found Emily and Hawk sitting out by a small fire.

"Good evening, Carman. What brings you out tonight?"

"I thought if you were not too busy, you might come stay with the child while I and Ward go down by the river."

"That moon up there got ya?"

"I don't know about that, Emily."

"Well, of course I'll stay with her."

"What about me?" asked Hawk, picking at a loose thread on his jacket.

"Now, Hawk, let's not you start raising a ruckus. If Carman and Ward want to go down by the river and watch the moon, I think that's just all right."

"If you say so," sputtered Hawk.

"Come on, Hawk. You're coming with me. We can sit and talk just as well over at Leaky's wagon as we can here."

"Well, I was thinking—"

"If you had anything on your mind, you should have said something before. Now get off your haunches and come with me."

Reluctantly, Hawk grunted and groaned while getting to his feet, then he followed Emily and Carman back to where Ward was waiting.

Coming near the campfire, Emily spotted the child and stopped dead in her tracks. "Just look at that. She's sound asleep."

Carman smiled, "She doesn't know the world is still going around."

"That would be kind of nice sometimes," replied Emily, dropping to her knees alongside the child. After a moment, she turned to Carman. "Now you two go to the river and come back when you're ready. This little girl is going to be just fine here with me."

"How about me?" asked Hawk, spinning a piece of rock between his fingers.

Emily smiled back at Hawk. "Yes, Hawk, you too."

Ward and Carman backed away then made their way to the river where they sat near the water's edge. There they looked out over the water where the moonlight reflected on the whitecaps and danced out of sight.

"It's a beautiful night, don't you think?" asked Carman, leaning her head on Ward's shoulder.

"Yes, and it's much more beautiful here with you."

"In the darkness, the river doesn't look or sound as violent as it did when we were trying to ford it," sighed Carman, stroking the back of Ward's hand.

"It would be almost peaceful if it weren't for the roar of the water charging down from the high country toward open water someplace far away."

"Do you think we're headed in the same direction of the water, Ward?"

"It's hard to tell." Ward reached up and placed his hand on Carman's soft hair gleaming in the moonlight. "You are beautiful, Carman."

"I'm glad you can't see my face."

"Why?"

"I believe I'm blushing." With that she turned and placed her moist lips to Ward's.

Ward took her in his arms and laid her on the soft green grass. The moonlight sparkled in her eyes. "You are beautiful, Carman, just beautiful. I don't know how our maker could have cast you from a mold created by man."

"Oh, Ward, you make me feel special."

"You're special, Carman. In my wildest dreams I never thought I would ever meet someone like you."

"You are very special to me, Ward; I hope you know that."

"How could I not help but know. The way you look at me, tells me more than words. I would like to tell you how much you mean to me, but there are not enough words that could express my real feelings.

Carman smiled up at Ward and rubbed his cheek with her gentle hand. "You just did."

"Did what?"

She reached out and took Ward by the hand. "You just told me how much you think of me."

Carman then pulled Ward down and he laid alongside her. With the moonlight shining on them and with the chorus from the rushing water they became engrossed in love's tenderness.

A kiss, a sigh, a touch. Time was kind to them as they were engulfed in a warm physical love that carried them into a world where neither of them had ever been before.

Drenched with perspiration, they became locked in each others arms. A certain weakness captured Carman and her arms dropped to her side.

Ward, breathless, lay down beside Carman and placed his hand on her cheek. "Are you all right?

"I have never been more right in my life, Ward."

"Nor have I."

"Others have told me of love, but I never dreamed it could be so fulfilling."

"I know," agreed Ward, still licking his parched lips.

"Are you satisfied?" asked Carman, rolling up on one elbow and rubbing her finger across Ward's chest.

"Oh, yes, are you?'

"I'm completely content. I have never experienced such peace and happiness."

Ward turned and looked up at the moon. "Will you ever forget this night, Carman?"

"Never. No matter whatever happens in my life, this will be the one night I'll always remember."

With time running out they walked slowly back to the wagon train. Upon entering the camp they found everything quiet. Ward checked the horses while Carman joined Emily. Emily with the Indian Child's head in her lap hummed a melody to her.

"Is she asleep?" asked Carman.

"She just drifted off. I think she missed you."

"That's wonderful to have someone want you."

Emily smiled as she slipped out from under the child's head and got to her feet. "I think you have two someones that care for you."

"You mean, Ward?"

"Well, of course I do and I think he's a fine young man. You two make such a nice couple."

Emily had just left when Ward joined Carman who was sitting with the child on a blanket just outside the wagon.

"How did they get along?" asked Ward, sitting down next to Carman.

"Just fine. That Emily could get along with a rattlesnake if she set her mind to it," commented Ward.

"How about Hawk?" smiled Ward.

"I think she has him tamed pretty well, don't you?"

Ward had a time not laughing out loud, but nodded in agreement with what Carman had said.

"It was wonderful, Ward."

"Yes, I know."

Carman had rolled over on her back and was looking into the moonlit night when she said. "I love you, Ward."

Ward looked into her moonstruck eyes. "That's saying a lot."

"I know and I mean it. I hope you have some feelings for me, but if you don't it still would not change the way I feel toward you."

Ward was without words for a moment, but then said. "I do have feelings for you, but I can't tell if it's love. I've never loved anyone before."

"Before!" exclaimed Carman, coming up on one elbow and looking Ward straight in the eyes. "Does that mean you love me?"

"I don't understand."

"You said you had never loved anyone before, so that means you love me."

Ward took her in his arms and kissed her. "If feeling the way I do is love, then I love you."

Carman melted in Ward's arms and sighed. "Those are the sweetest words I've ever heard."

The rest of the evening was filled with words of love and plans for the future. When it was time to turn in, they placed the Indian Child between them to keep her warm during the night.

CHAPTER FIFTEEN

ROLLING PLAINS OF LUSH GREEN grass drenched with dew sparkled in the morning sun. The air, however, was hot and heavy, making it difficult for man and beast to breathe. A lather like sweat covered the horses' backs and sides as they pulled their loads.

Thunderheads had been building in the west since before noon. By 3:00 p.m. hideous black clouds were on the ground sweeping across the plains. Thunder rolled and lightning streaked across the skies and to the ground. The full force of the storm was not far off.

Hawk looked up in time to see Leaky standing in his wagon. Sending his whip out over his mules, Leaky was yelling at the top of his voice.

Hawk struck out to meet him. "What is it?" shouted Hawk.

"Buffalo. A herd of buffalo has stampeded and they are heading in our direction. There has got to be hundreds of them. If we don't do something, they'll go through these wagons without knowing it."

Ward seeing Leaky yelling and waving his arms rode out to join Hawk. "What is it?"

Hawk whirled around. "A herd of buffalo has stampeded. They're heading in our direction."

"From what direction?" shouted out Ward.

"The north. Now turn this train south in single file, that's if you have the time. I don't want them to broadside us or they'll wipe us out."

"What happened?" shouted Ward.

"It's the storm. Get those wagons turned and have the men ready with their rifles; we're going to need them. We'll have to drop as many of the buffalo as possible in order to have any chance of turning them."

Ward rode out shouting, "Get these wagons headed south in single file or we'll all be killed! Now hurry it up."

Men on their wagons, gripping the reins with one hand and their whips with the other, brought their teams around on the dead run and lined them up. The train had just made the turn and was heading south when over the crest of a hill to the north, came the thundering herd of buffalo. With their heads down they were running hard. Lightning streaked to the ground causing the animals to run without caution. A cloud of dust and clods of dirt rose up from their hammering hooves.

Hawk with his rifle over one arm rode hard toward the herd then turned and came up alongside, firing at the lead bulls. One by one they dropped.

Ward, seeing what Hawk was doing, rode out and began firing, dropping buffalo one by one. Fire erupted from the guns of the settlers still on their wagons, but still the buffalo came. Approaching the wagons, suddenly the herd split and roared on by. Teams of horses thrashed around in their harness. Some became entangled and dropped to the ground. Following the herd of buffalo, there came a downpour of rain. Lightning lashed at the ground like an angry serpent's tongue sending further fear through the fainthearted.

With the herd disappearing into the stormy darkness, Ward and Hawk joined the others to see how everyone had come through the ordeal. The men were trying to settle down their teams and cattle, while the women held their crying children in their arms.

Hawk rode up to Emily who was at the head of her lead team, patting their faces and stroking their manes. "How did you come out?" asked Hawk.

" I think I'm altogether, but I'm going to tell you one thing."

" What's that?"

" I thought I was fearless, but this came close to sending me into a tizzy."

Hawk removed his hat and clawed at his hair. "This is the first time I've ever had this happen. I've heard others tell about it, but I never thought it could be so damn frightening."

"Were you frightened?" asked Emily, still working with her teams.

"Not really, but if anyone tells me they were frightened, I will not say a word about it. This was good cause to be scared to death."

Ward had joined Carman and was looking into her eyes filled with fear "Are they coming back, Ward?"

"No, Carman. This storm is apt to chase that herd off the face of the earth."

Carman on the ground pointed to the Indian Child sitting on the wagon seat with her legs swinging back and forth.

"Do I see a slight smile on her face?" asked Ward, staring sternly at the child.

" Yes, and she was laughing out loud all the while the herd was thundering by."

"It's hard to believe."

"It's true."

"Oh, Carman, I don't doubt you. That was just a figure of speech."

Moments later Hawk rode up. "How did you stand it, Carman?"

"It took a lot out of me, but we made it.

Ward still overwhelmed with the way the Indian Child reacted, said to Hawk, "Carman tells me the child laughed most of the time the buffalo were running by her."

"That doesn't surprise me."

"How could that be, Hawk? That was one hell of a frightening experience. I'm sure the other children won't sleep because of it."

"They're not Indians, either."

Ward, strong in his reply said, "What does that have to do with being frightened?"

"A lot, Ward. The Indian is close to these animals. They grow up to respect the brutes, but they're not afraid of them. They give the Indian food, leather, blankets and the list goes on. Their children are taught to respect them. There isn't much the buffalo can do to create anger in the minds and hearts of the Indian."

"I guess I understand."

Hawk gave Ward a wave and rode off. By that time, large drops of rain were falling to earth. Hurriedly Ward helped Carman and the child into the wagon and then joined them. Darkened skies opened up once more. Wind and rain lashed at the canvas covering the wagon. They sat without talking for it was impossible to hear over the torrent of rain that was falling. Gusting winds snapped the canvas flaps, making them sound like rifle shots. The Indian Child had found her sock doll and was playing with it during the height of the storm. Carman looked on, shaking her head in disbelief.

After the storm subsided, Ward threw open the front flap and looked out. The black cloud to the north had opened up. Welcome sun rays were streaming through. "Come out, Carman. The air is fresh and clean."

Carman appeared in the canvas opening, looked up and smiled. "How can it be so violent one minute and so serene the next?"

"I don't know," replied Ward, "but it will be a long time before I forget what happened here this afternoon."

While standing next to the wagon seat, Carman spoke in a low voice. "Did you see the way the little one reacted to the storm while we were in the wagon?"

"Yes, Carman, I did and it all goes back to her life in the wild."

It was nearly an hour before Hawk appeared at the head of the wagon train. "Come on, you bunch of hardy souls. We're moving out."

CHAPTER SIXTEEN

DAYS PASSED LIKE WEEKS as the wagon train ground its way over and through the many perils. There had been further loses of livestock and wagons. Many of the settlers walked the trail carrying the only thing they owned and that was a heavy heart in their chest. They were strong people looking only to the West and what it would hold for them.

It was mid-afternoon when Hawk rode the full length of the train shouting, "We're making camp here. Leave your wagons right where they are; there's no need to circle them tonight."

"What are we stopping for now?" asked Ward, trotting his horse up to Hawk.

"They're tired, Ward, every last one of them and I don't think they know how tired they are."

"That's possible."

"Damn right it's possible; just look to the east."

"Yes?"

"Look at the mountains there behind us," said Hawk, nodding toward the towering peaks.

"I don't know what you're getting at, Hawk. Just tell me."

"You're like the rest, Ward. You don't realize that we have just crossed her majesty the mountain."

Ward pushed his hat back and gazed at the high peaks, shear walls and jagged slopes. "Well, I'll be."

"Yes, Ward, when you're so close to the mountains, you can't see them. You don't realize how massive they are. If we could, no one would ever attempt to cross them."

"You're like a fox, Hawk. You seem to have your hand on everything regardless of what some of us might think from time to time."

Hawk smiled. "It's all right, Ward. I understand."

Ward rode back to where Carman, the child and Leaky were standing at Leaky's wagon. "What's up, Ward?" asked Leaky.

"Hawk just wants to give everyone a little more rest today and tonight. It has been a long haul the last few days, so he thought it was time for all of us to relax before going on in the morning."

Carman looked up at Ward. "Those who are walking are very weary. I didn't think Hawk could see that, but I guess he did."

"The man doesn't miss much, Carman," joined in Leaky, brushing the dust off the brim of his hat.

The last few days and nights had been cold and now the sun was warm. The breeze was without a chill and they were able to strip themselves of jackets, sweaters and enjoy the warmth.

"Wonder why Hawk didn't have us make a circle tonight?" asked Carman.

"I don't know and I don't question Hawk's judgment too often."

Leaky entered into the conversation, "Sometimes you do."

"Sometimes I do what?"

"You question Hawk."

"Well, yes, but generally Hawk is right in what he does. He's a wise man when it comes to this trail."

Ward hadn't heard Emily come up behind him, but he did know she was there when she blurted out. "Yes, and that's the only thing that man knows anything about."

Ward turned and smiled at Emily. "You know, Emily, I wonder why Hawk lets you come on the trail with him."

"Don't tell me that, Ward. You know as well as I do why I'm here."

Ward chuckled, "Well, maybe I do."

Carman supported a grin from ear to ear and Leaky just kicked at the ground with the toe of his boot.

Emily sidled up to Carman. "You don't need someone to look after the child do you?"

"No, Emily, but if you want to take her for a while, you

are welcome to do so. I think she likes you."

"Do you really?" asked Emily, waiting eagerly for Carman to turn the child over to her.

"Well, of course I do. Hasn't she always been good for you?" inquired Carman.

"Yes, I guess she has. I do know she has put some joy in this trip for me," smiled Emily, reaching for the child's extended hand.

"You see, Emily, she wants to go to you."

"I think she does."

Carman smiled in Ward's direction then looked back at Emily who was on her knees running her fingers through the child's straight black hair. "Like I said, Emily, she may go with you. If you need me we'll be right around here. Right, Ward?"

"Yes, we'll be here all right," agreed Ward.

Emily's heart was on her sleeve for the way she looked at the Indian Child was with warmth and kindness.

Carman grasp Ward's hands in hers while watching Emily with the child walk with pride among the settlers.

Emily seemed to be the only one moving about. The settlers just knowing that Hawk realized they were all very weary, took the time to lay around and rest their aching bodies and troubled minds.

As the sun's last rays streaked across the skies, Ward glanced up. There in the shadowed light was Hawk, Emily and the Indian Child looking toward the west.

"What you looking at, Hawk?" asked Emily.

"Don't really know," he replied, "but it just seems this trip has been different than the rest."

"In what way?"

"I can't put my hand on it—it's just different."

"The least you could do is tell me."

"Nope, Emily, because I don't know myself."

"You're talking in circles, Hawk and that's not like you."

"You know, Emily, I've come over this trail more times than I would like to think about and where has it got me. I bring these settlers out here and give them a new start, then I return to Hannibal and take the lead again. Doesn't seem like much of a life does it.?"

Emily bent down and picked the child up. "No, Hawk,

and I don't know how long I can keep coming across with you."

"I know and that worries me too."

"How's that?" asked Emily, looking at Hawk, never seeing him so humble.

"I don't know what I would do if you told me you wouldn't be with me on the next trip."

"You know I'll be coming across hell's trail as long as you do and I'm able."

"I know that, Emily, but that's not fair to you either."

"I've gotten over thinking about myself, Hawk."

"And I guess I don't have to think too much about it to know you have put me ahead of your dreams."

"That's all right, we all have to give and take a little."

Hawk raised his voice some. "A little, well I guess so. You've been giving and I've been taking ."

"Maybe it has been a little lopsided, but I'm not complaining."

Hawk whirled around and took Emily in his arms. "You know, Emily, I'm going to give you something to think about."

"What's that?"

"You have a choice to make when we get to our destination."

"I do?"

"Yep. We can either stay out here or go back to Hannibal and settle down there."

"You asking me to marry you, Hawk?"

"Don't know, but just think about what I said. Now don't you be telling me what you decide until the time comes and we sit down and talk about it."

Emily smiled back at Hawk. "It's a good thing other women don't know you like I do or I'd have to fight them off."

"Shucks, Emily."

"Guess I better take the child back to Carman. They'll be wondering where I've run off to."

"Can I see you later, Emily?"

"Just come around to the wagon and I'll be there."

Emily, with the child in her arms, returned to Carman who was sitting with Ward and Leaky beside a cheery fire crackling under a pot of hot soup. "Something smells awful good, Carman."

"Leaky shot a rabbit this afternoon, so that's what we're having for supper tonight."

"Sure smells good."

"How was the little one for you?" inquired Carman.

"Just fine, look at the way she has her head on my shoulder."

"I noticed," said Carman, reaching out for the child. The child lifted her head and looked into Emily's eyes.

Emily's eyes mellowed, "You must go to Carman."

The child brought both hands up under her chin. "Come, on, honey," said Carman. "It's almost time for bed."

Emily handed the child to Carman and stepped back. "You know, Carman, I think this might be one of the happiest days of my life. But please don't ask me why."

"That's not fair, Emily. Now you have me wondering."

"I guess you'll have to wonder awhile longer, but someday I promise I'll tell you."

The child squirmed in Carman's arms when Emily turned and walked away. "This child sure has taken to Emily."

"I see that," said Ward.

CHAPTER SEVENTEEN

AFTER A RESTFUL AFTERNOON and night, the settlers were up before daybreak. The women were preparing breakfast while the men were hitching their teams to the wagons.

Hawk didn't seem to be in such a yank as he had been other mornings and this puzzled many of the settlers, including Ward.

Ward left Carman and walked up to Hawk who was looking out over the wagon train. "What's the matter, Hawk?" asked Ward.

"Nothing, why?"

"I haven't heard you shouting out orders this morning."

"Maybe I'm just tired of shouting out orders, Ward."

"You got a down day coming up?"

"Don't think so."

Ward pushed his hat forward. "Everyone is anxious to get on the trail, Hawk, except you."

"I expect they are, but what would you say if I told you I wasn't all that anxious for this trip to end."

"I wouldn't know what to say."

"Well, that's what I'm telling you."

"But why, Hawk?"

"Now don't be telling anyone, but this may be my last trip."

"I can't hardly believe that, Hawk."

"It's the truth. Something about this trip just took a lot out of me."

"What does Emily think about that?" asked Ward.

"What's she got to say about anything I want to do?" growled Hawk, glancing harshly at Ward.

Ward smiled only to himself. "Probably nothing."

"That's right and I wouldn't want anyone to think that she has anything to do with running this train or my life."

"I'm sure no one would ever think that, Hawk. You're too tough to have a woman interfere with your life."

"You got that right."

"Is there anything I can do?" asked Ward, looking at Hawk with concern.

"Nope. I guess it's like you were saying, I must be having a bad day." With that, Hawk turned, and his booming voice rang out. "Move 'em out; we can't expect to get anywhere if we sit here all day!"

Horses, mules and oxen hit their collars and the train moved forward. The settlers after a good night's rest were refreshed. The steps of those who were walking were quick and the children laughed and played.

An hour or so had passed when Mr. Hineburg thundered back to the train. Excitement rang in his voice when he stammered, "Hawk, just over that knoll up there...."

"Yes, Mr. Hineburg, are you trying to tell me you have never seen a valley quite so green or flat or wide?"

"Yes, that's what I'm trying to say."

"You're right, Mr. Hineburg. I don't believe there's a more beautiful spread in the world, but keep it to yourself. I want everyone to experience the same excitement as you are now."

"I won't say a thing. I'm going back out."

Hawk smiled to himself for he always looked forward to this time during each trip.

Shortly thereafter, the first wagon broke over the crest of a knoll. Mr. Hineburg had returned and was sitting tall in his saddle watching the faces of each settler as their wagons moved past him. Roars went up from some, while others looked on in amazement and disbelief. As the last wagon, that being Leaky, broke over the knoll, Hawk yelled at the top of his voice, "Hold 'em up, men; hold 'em up!"

The teams came to a halt, allowing the settlers to look out over the vast expanse. As far as the eye could see it was green and lush. Those on the wagons dropped to the ground and with the others walked up to where Hawk was standing.

Seeing that all the settlers were there, Hawk turned and

addressed them. "Well, folks, you're almost there compared to where we started. It will be several days before we arrive at our destination, but the going is easy and fears should no longer capture your every thought. I'm darn proud of all of you; you're a fine bunch of people with grit like I've never seen before." Hawk hesitated and then went on. "I would like to have you turn around and look back."

As one, they turned and were looking back. Hawk continued, "You see those mountains over there?"

A mumbled response came forth. "Well, I'm here to tell you that you have just come through them. Now imagine if you would have known that each step was taking you through her majesty, would you have had the courage to go on? I would guess that most of you would still be back in Hannibal."

One of the women moaned then sank to the ground. "What's the matter with her?" asked Hawk.

"She fainted, can't you see that?" shouted Emily, rushing to her side.

"What for?"

Ward joined in. "You know, Hawk, to look back and realize that we've just come up, over and around those giants is pretty darn humbling."

"Can't see that."

"You mean to tell me you were not overwhelmed with your first trip out here?"

"Maybe a little."

"You're darn right he was, Ward, and don't you let him tell you anything different. I know; I was with him." It was Emily who had left the woman in the hands of her husband and had come up behind Hawk.

"Damn it, Emily, will you stop sneaking up on me like some animal after their prey."

Carman with the Indian Child on her hip joined Ward. "It's just beautiful, isn't it?"

"Beautiful seems rather shallow to describe the mountains," remarked Ward, slipping his arm around Carman.

Carman glanced up at Ward. "Will it be the same when we arrive at our destination?"

Ward looked into Carman's dreamy eyes. "Not unless you want it to change."

"Oh, no Ward, nothing like that," she replied, hugging the Indian Child and kissing her forehead.

Emily turned to Carman and reached out for the child. "Here, would you like to hold her?" asked Carman.

"May I?"

"Why, of course you may. You don't need to ask," smiled Carman, handing the child to Emily.

Out of the crowd came a strong voice asking, "When can we expect to be at our destination?" It was Leaky, after he had removed the large cud of tobacco from his mouth.

"It will be a few more days, but they'll go by fast."

"Can't be to soon for me, Hawk."

"You've been doing pretty good, Leaky. Now don't you get so anxious you can't do your job back there."

"Don't worry about that. And by the way, it doesn't look like I'm going to have to eat sand much longer."

"You're right, Leaky. Now let's everyone get back to their wagons and we'll head out of here."

A shout went up as the settlers hurried back to their wagons and waited for Hawk to give them the word.

Looking back and giving Leaky a wave, Hawk bellowed out, "Anyone want to go to San Francisco?"

"Yes!" was the roar that went up.

"Then let's get 'em moving."

Ward rode along with Hawk, while Carman and the child rode alongside Emily.

After a short time Emily asked, "You and Ward have any plans for when we get to San Francisco?"

"I have, but I still am not sure about Ward," replied Carman, smiling out of the corner of her mouth.

Emily, looking brighter than usual, commented, "I just can't understand these men sometimes. You can lay your body and soul down in front of them and still they are not sure they love you."

"I had the same feeling, so it's really no different from one to the other."

"As far as I'm concerned, there's no difference."

Carman laughed then stopped her horse. She waited for Leaky to come forward, so that she could ride with him and keep him company. It had been a long and lonely journey for Leaky, but as a loner by nature he handled it well.

"What you going to do, Leaky, when this trip is all over?"

"Oh, I might pan a little gold if I have enough money to buy a pan, a donkey and a stake."

"You going to have enough?" asked Carman, brushing the hair out of the child's eyes.

"I reckon I will, as long as I stay out of the first saloon I come to."

"I'll stay with you until you get over the rough spots and see you on your way into the mountains," said Carman.

"That's mighty decent of you, but I hope I'm man enough to hold out. I've always wanted to come out here and I wouldn't do anything to disappoint Ward."

"Ward?" was Carman's questioning response.

"Yes, he had enough faith in me to get me this job with Hawk."

"Where did he meet up with you?"

"Where else but a saloon and I was half-drunk then."

"Do you think you owe Ward something for having faith in you?"

"You're darn right I do. He is the only person since my mother that had any faith in me and then I let her down."

"What are you kicking yourself around for, Leaky?"

"I don't know. Guess I'm feeling sorry for myself right about now."

"Look at Mr. Hineburg, Mr. Strong and Mrs. Worton. They all had someone when they left and they were taken away," said Carman.

Leaky hesitated, then looked up.

Carman sputtered, "But you, you had nothing, so you only have one way to go and that's up."

Leaky bit his lip. "I expect you're right. So I guess I can just stop my whimpering, especially when I know my downfall was my own fault."

"I didn't say that, but no doubt you're right."

Carman with the child on her lap rode on to where Ward was at and stayed with him for most of the day.

CHAPTER EIGHTEEN

THE NEXT FEW DAYS were filled with hope and thanksgiving. Those who had lost loved ones along the way had regained their strength and were more determined than ever to see it through, if not for themselves for the sake of those they had lost. Even Mr. Hineburg and Mrs. Worton had been seen taking their meals together and enjoying what free time they had.

After making camp one night and before supper, Hawk called the settlers together. They assembled quickly for they were eager to find out what Hawk had to say.

"Well, this is it, ladies and gentlemen. Tomorrow we'll be rolling into San Francisco. There won't be any welcoming party when we arrive. After you go on about your way, many of you will be swallowed up in the hustle of the city, while others of you will meet with success. All I can say is there are the best people you'll ever want to meet out here and there are the worst, so tread easily and do not be sucked in by some fast talking dude from the cities back East, do you hear me?"

Out of the crowd strolled a man who had been traveling alone and had had very little to do with the rest of the settlers.

Approaching Hawk, he spoke up, "Hawk is right in what he just said about the best and the worst of the people. You're the best and I'm on the other side. I'm sure you've noticed I've spent my time alone and there was a reason for that. I am a gunfighter and if someone crosses me, I'm apt to drop them dead in their tracks. Therefore, I avoided any confrontation with any of you. Now just a word, do not cross anyone just for the sake of pride. It may be a deadly mistake on your part."

With that, the man faded into the crowd and returned to his wagon.

Hawk rubbed his wiry beard and said, "I guess he said it better than I did. If I were you, I would heed his warning. Who knows, you might just meet up with him on the street or in some wayward saloon."

The crowd disbursed and Carman stood staring at the ground ahead of her. "Ward, did you hear that? We'll be arriving in San Francisco tomorrow."

"Sounds like it."

"Well?"

"Well, what?"

"Are you going to be swallowed up in the hustle of the city?"

"No, Carman. Once we get there we will find a place where we can be alone and we can decide what to do then."

"Can we do that tonight?"

"Well, I guess."

Carman clutching the Indian Child whispered, "Can't we do it now?"

"Let's wait until we have supper, then we can talk."

Before Carman could answer, Emily walked up alongside her. "May I have the child for a while?"

"Well, of course you may," replied Carman. The child reached out for Emily and Emily took her in her arms.

"This will be my last night with her; would you mind if she stayed with me?"

"I have no objections. Do you, Ward?" asked Carman.

"Not at all."

Emily left with the child looking over her shoulder.

Leaky, with his mules and wagon, pulled up alongside Ward and Carman. "Why are you looking so long faced; ain't tomorrow what you been looking for?"

"I don't really know," said Carman, reaching for Ward's hand.

"How about you, Ward?"

"Guess this is the place that I want to be."

"Well, I know it is where I want to be and I can just smell those gold nuggets out there."

"You're serious about looking for gold, aren't you?" asked Ward.

"You bet I am. What else could I do with all these young bucks out here to compete with?"

"You may have a point, Leaky, but it's not going to be an easy life."

"I'll bet it's going to be easier than hanging over a bar half-drunk all day long," replied Leaky.

Carman smiled, "I'm sure you were not that bad."

"Oh, but I was. If it hadn't been for Ward, I would be there yet. Ask Ward what a hell of a mess I was when he found me."

Ward shrugged his shoulders. "He was in pretty bad shape, Carman."

"How come you took an interest in Leaky?" inquired Carman, looking through questioning eyes.

"I didn't like the way he was being treated, that's why."

"Ward's a good man, Carman. Don't let him go," said Leaky.

"I'm trying not to."

"Enough of this," said Ward. "I'm going to start a fire."

"Then I'll get some side pork around, is that all right?" joked Leaky.

"What else is there?" inquired Carman.

Leaky's smile widened, "Nothing."

Carman laughed out loud, "I thought so."

After they had eaten and darkness had moved in, Ward and Carman slipped away, finding a place where they could be alone.

"Can you just hold me in your arms tonight, Ward?"

"Why, yes, if that's what you want."

"I'd like that."

Ward held Carman while they lay on the ground looking up into the jeweled-like sky. "I wonder if the stars look the same back East?" asked Carman, snuggling down in Ward's arms.

"I would suppose so."

"Are you angry that I just want to be held?"

"No, Carman. What would make you say a thing like that?"

"I was just wondering."

"Then wonder about the things that need wondering about."

"All right," agreed Carman, smiling to herself.

They were both laying on their backs when Ward spoke up, "Carman."

"Yes?"

"Will you marry me?"

Carman lifted herself up slowly and looked into Ward's face. "You just asked me to marry you."

"Yes, I did."

"Well, what am I supposed to say?"

"Yes would be plenty."

"Well, of course," Carman paused and patted her chest. "Yes, Ward, I'll marry you. I love you, Ward, and I was so afraid we would go our separate ways once we got out here."

"No, Carman. If you'll have me, we'll go away together."

Leaning forward she kissed Ward. Her lips were soft and moist. "I'm awake aren't I?"

"Yes, Carman, you're awake."

"Hold me, Ward, and don't ever let me go."

It was nearly time for them to return to the wagon train when Ward said, "I have something I want to talk to you about and I don't know how you're going to take it."

"You will never know unless you ask, will you?"

"It's the Indian Child."

Carman sat up. "Yes, what about her?"

"We're young, Carman, and we will be young for a long time."

"What are you getting at?"

Ward wiped the perspiration from around his neck with his hand. "We'll have children of our own, but Emily will never have children."

"What are you suggesting?"

"I think we should turn the child over to her. It will be the only chance she'll ever have."

"I've thought about that, but I don't know if I could bring myself to do it. I would be letting the child down. She depends on me, Ward."

"I know and that's why we are talking about it. The child loves Emily and that you cannot deny."

"I know, and Emily loves her."

"Then what do you think?"

"Can I answer that in the morning? What if Emily would say no?"

"Then we would keep the child," replied Ward.

Carman threw her arms around his neck. "You are a wonderful man, Ward. How come I'm so lucky?"

With Carman on Ward's arm, they returned to camp where they found Emily playing with the child under the wagon.

"What are you doing under there?" inquired Carman smiling warmly.

"This is where she wanted to play, so this is where we are playing."

Ward looked at Carman and chuckled. Hawk was sitting on Emily's wagon tongue, his legs crossed and with a long face indeed. "What's the matter with you, Hawk?"

"Nothing, why?"

"You look like you have lost your best friend."

"Oh, Lord," chirped in Emily. "He is so jealous of this child he can't see straight."

"Now Emily, that's not true and you know it," growled Hawk, looking back at her in disgust.

"Well, if I'm going to keep peace in the camp, I had better be paying some attention to Hawk," grunted Emily, crawling out from under the wagon on her hands and knees, followed by the child.

"Come on, little one," said Carman, holding her hands out.

The child jumped to her feet and looked at Emily. Emily motioned for her to go to Carman, but instead the child wrapped her arms around Emily's neck and held on tightly.

"I guess she wants to stay with you tonight," said Carman.

"She can if you don't mind," was Emily's eager response.

"If she won't be any bother, I guess it's all right," Carman swallowed hard and looked at Ward. He nodded his head slightly and took Carman by her quivering arm. "Shall we go?"

"If you need me, I'll be by the fire," said Carman, leaving with Ward.

Upon returning to Leaky's wagon, Ward said, "Emily may have a problem with the two children tonight."

"Two?"

"Yes, Hawk and the little one."

Carman roared with laughter and held her sides. "I never thought about that, but I think you're right."

CHAPTER NINETEEN

MORNING CAME WITH A BLAZING red sun peeking over the mountains to the east. The settlers were out before dawn in anticipation of the last day of their grueling trip from Hannibal. Hawk roamed the campsite, speaking and talking with anyone who might have the time.

Stopping off at Mrs. Worton's wagon, Hawk said, "My, you look nice this morning—not that you don't look nice every morning."

"Well, thank you, Hawk. It was nice of you to stop by." She paused for a moment, then spoke softly, "I don't want everyone to know, but Mr. Hineburg and I are planning on being married as soon as we arrive in San Francisco."

"That's wonderful, Mrs. Worton, if that's what you want."

"Oh, yes, it's what we both want."

"I'd say you are both very lucky, Mrs. Worton. Mr. Hineburg is a strong, but gentle man and he couldn't have found a finer woman than you are."

"I guess maybe you are someone I didn't know while we were on the trail. You seem so different."

Hawk grinned. "A pretty wrapped gift at a party isn't always the best one when you look inside."

Mrs. Worton laughed, "Hawk, you are a devil."

"If I don't have time to talk with you again, do have a good life"

"I will and thank you."

As Hawk started to leave, Mrs. Worton said, "Oh, yes. I don't care if Emily and Carman know about Mr. Hineburg and me, but I don't care about everyone knowing."

"Good day, Mrs. Worton," said Hawk, tipping his hat.

Like a woman at a quilting bee, Hawk hurried over to

Emily's wagon and told her about Mrs. Worton and Mr. Hineburg.

Emily raised her hands, "Glory be, this is wonderful news! Let's go tell Carman."

"All right, but only you and Carman are to know."

"Why is that?"

"I don't know, Emily. All I know is that Mrs. Worton doesn't want anyone else to know."

Carman and Ward were together, so Emily told them about Mrs. Worton and Mr. Hineburg and expressed Mrs. Worton's wishes.

Carman beamed all over. "That's wonderful news, Emily. I think they're just made for each other."

"Do you suppose its fate, them getting to know each other this way?"

Hawk was rather sharp when he said, "Oh, come on, Emily"

"You never know about such things."

After Hawk and Emily quieted down, Ward expressed his happiness for Mrs. Worton and Mr. Hineburg.

The sun had cleared the mountains. The air was fresh and a sparkling blue sky was overhead.

Ward had no more than told Carman they should be moving out soon, when out of the silence came Hawk's booming voice. "All right, folks. We are on our last leg, so let's move 'em out!"

Shouts went up. Tears streaked some of their faces. Happiness captured most of their lives, while others mourned their losses. The wagons rolled on toward their final destination.

It was three that afternoon when the wagon train with its weary travelers rolled into San Francisco and stopped. Hawk quickly gathered everyone around him.

"This is the end of the trail folks, so from here on you are on your own. Be aware of the scoundrels out here and don't fall for anything that sounds too good to be true. The only one making money in a fast scheme is the hustler. He can duke you out of your money before you can blink an eye. Now, good luck!"

Mrs. Worton had slipped her hand into Mr. Hineburg's hand and smiled slightly. "It doesn't seem possible. This is like being born again. There's really nothing left of our lives as we knew it when we moved out of Hannibal."

"No, but I'm happy with what we have," smiled Mr. Hineburg, squeezing Mrs. Worton's hand softly.

In the meantime, Carman and Ward had located Emily standing next to her wagon.

"Emily."

"Oh, yes, Carman, I was hoping I would see you before you left."

Ward stepped forward. "What are you going to do from here on?"

"I was hoping Hawk would ask me to marry him, but I think he got off the hook again."

A large shadow appeared over Emily's shoulder. She turned around to see Hawk smiling down on her. "Would you like to marry me, Emily? You just said you wanted to."

Emily's knees buckled, but Ward caught her before she went down.

Hawk reached for Emily and brought her to him. Ward and Carman were happy being a part of Emily's happiest day.

"Yes, Hawk, I'll marry you and I'll wait for you to set the date. I'm sure you won't want to rush into this."

"You have waited long enough, so we'll marry tomorrow."

"That soon?" asked Emily. "I don't know that I can be ready."

"Don't give me too much time, Emily. I might back out."

Emily still beaming spoke up. "What time tomorrow?"

Both Carman and Ward snickered to themselves as they watched and listened to the two of them spar with each other.

After Hawk and Emily had settled down some, Carman took Emily by the hands. "Emily, Ward and I have been talking and have come up with something that could involve you."

"Yes?"

"The Indian Child."

"What about her?" exclaimed Emily.

"Ward and I are young and we intend to raise a family of our own, so we were wondering if maybe you would like to take the Indian Child with you and raise her as your own. She does love you."

Tears flowed down Carman's cheeks and Ward had to turn away.

"I think I might have something to say about this, Carman," said Hawk, throwing his shoulders back.

"No, Hawk, there is only one thing to say. I want her," wept Emily, reaching out for the child still standing alongside Carman.

The child looked up at Carman. Carman placed her hand in the center of the child's back and guided her to Emily. Hawk and Ward stepped aside and let Emily and the child caress each other.

Emily looked up through tear soaked eyes, "Do you know what you have just done?"

Carman smiled, still biting her lip, "I've done the right thing."

"Oh, yes, Carman. I'll raise her to be a lady and she will be beautiful."

Ward uneasily said, "We must go, Carman."

"I'll be just a minute."

Carman ran to Leaky's wagon and came back with the sock doll she had made for the child. "Here, I wouldn't want to leave before giving this to her. It's really the only thing she has to her name."

Carman dropped to her knees and handed the child her doll. "I love you, little one. I'm doing the right thing by you. Emily will love and care for you like your own mother."

Quickly, Carman jumped to her feet and ran over to Ward. "Please, Ward—take me away. I don't want to look back."

THE END